Dmitry's Royal Flush:

Rise of the Queen

DRF

Latrivia S. Nelson

RiverHouse Publishing, LLC
9160 Highway 64
Suite 12, #176
Lakeland, TN 38002

All **RiverHouse, LLC** Titles, Imprints and Distributed Lines are available at special quantity discounts for bulk purchases for sales promotions, premiums, fund-raising and educational or institutional use.

First RiverHouse, LLC Trade Paperback Printing: 07/01/2010

1

Imprint: *RiverHouse Publishing, LLC*

ISBN: **978-0578060118** *(sc)*

Printed in the United States
Memphis, Tennessee

This book is printed on acid-free paper.

www.riverhousepublishingllc.com

For Adam
Thanks for being just you.

Acknowledgments

There would be no Anya without Tierra and Jordan's constant inspiration. Thanks for being great teachers of the art of childhood for Mommy and Daddy each and every day.

To my world travelers, Adam and Markum, thank you for your continued insight.

To my blog readers who have been kind enough to have frank, open conversations with me about their lives, I am honored.

To every fan and every reader who supports my aspirations, thank you for believing in me.

Enjoy!

!!!Warning!!!

This book contains graphic violence, explicit sex, rape, murder, vulgar language and is only intended for adults over the age of 18. If you are not 18 or you wish to prevent the transfer of this kind of content to your psyche, please do not proceed. For those who have the stomach and meet the minimum age requirement, enjoy.

Rated: R

The Code

The Thieves' Code

A thief is bound by the Code to:

1. Forsake his relatives--mother, father, brothers, sisters...
2. Not have a family of his own -- no wife, no children; this does not however, preclude him from having a lover.
3. Never, under any circumstances work, no matter how much difficulty this brings. Live only on means gleaned from thievery.
4. Help other thieves -- both by moral and material support, utilizing the commune of thieves.
5. Keep secret information about the whereabouts of accomplices (i.e. dens, districts, hideouts, safe apartments, etc.).
6. In unavoidable situations (if a thief is under investigation) to take the blame for someone else's crime; this buys the other person time of freedom.
7. Demand a convocation of inquiry for the purpose of resolving disputes in the event of a conflict between oneself and other thieves or between thieves.
8. If necessary, participate in such inquiries.
9. Carry out the punishment of the offending thief as decided by the convocation.
10. Not resist carrying out the decision of punishing the offending thief who is found guilty, with punishment determined by the con-vocation.
11. Have good command of the thieves' jargon ("Fehnay").
12. Not gamble without being able to cover losses.
13. Teach the trade to young beginners.
14. Have, if possible, informants from the rank and file of thieves.
15. Not lose your reasoning ability when using alcohol.
16. Have nothing to do with the authorities (particularly with the ITU [Correctional Labor Authority]), not participate in public activities, nor join any community organizations.
17. Not take weapons from the hands of authorities; not serve in the military.
18. Make good on promises given to other thieves.

Prologue

There was a complete media frenzy behind the bomb attack on Mother Russia and the Medlov compound. Outlets from across the nation stood outside of the gates of Dmitry's home discussing the murder of a young, female shopkeeper and the attempted assassination of a millionaire of questionable character with alleged ties to the Vory v Zakone by his crime boss brother, Ivan Medlov, who headed the Memphis Medlov Organized Crime Family.

Obviously, the media had it all wrong, which was good for the men who had survived the attack and for his son, who was now the head of the family, but it was not good for his most apparent and haunting dilemma.

For nearly 15 years, Dmitry avoided his name ever making one newspaper regarding his possible connections to the mafia, and now his face was splashed across CNN, MSNBC and Fox News along with newspapers nationwide. He had no choice. He had to leave.

Three months had passed and although the house repaired and the restaurant rebuilt, there were several undercover investigations underway by the MPD, FBI, ICE, DEA and the IRS.

Dmitry was embattled, yet none of his worries outweighed the pain he felt for Royal.

He sat in the back of the limo as it escorted him now to the private airstrip, where he had made arrangements to fly to Prague to his new luxury villa that awaited him with a full staff and a newer life.

He also had purchased two large storefronts in the middle of Prague 1 district, where he had already started a new restaurant and an upscale clothing store called Royal Flush, just as he had promised *her*.

A staff had already been picked, and both would be open within the week. Besides, he had done everything that he could here. Dmitry's Closet and Mother Russia belonged to Anatoly now. There was nothing more to fix, no more reason to linger.

"What are you thinking about?" Royal asked, taking off her shades.

Dmitry put his hand on her knee and sighed. "You. This is big move so early in your recovery. I'm not sure that you even need to be out of bed."

"I'm ready." She rubbed her growing stomach. "I think we both are. This place is just a memory now. It's time to move and time for you to stop treating me like I'm made of glass."

The diamonds sparkled from her neck. Dmitry had purchased a three-million dollar diamond necklace, designed specifically to cover the large knife mark that Ivan had left when he tried to claim her life.

"Prague is a good change. A place where no one knows me or you," she said confidently. "I can feel it. Everything is going to be fine."

Dmitry raised his brow. "They know me, but there is no need to worry. I won't be boss in Czech Republic. I'll be shop keeper like you."

"Well, we'll finally have something in common."

The limo stopped on the airstrip, and the driver opened the door.

"Mrs. Medlov," he said, offering his hand.

"Umm, I never get tired of hearing that name," Royal said, taking his hand and smiling.

"Good, because you're going to hear it for the rest of your life." Dmitry stepped out after her.

There was not one cloud in the sky. Spring had brought fresh clean air, warm weather and unexplainable beauty with it. Memphis was wonderful that way, always offering all four seasons in full. Royal would miss that.

As soon as the sun hit Royal's necklace, it lit up the airstrip. Dmitry smiled. No matter where she went for the rest of her days, he would make sure that her lifestyle reflected her name. She would live like a queen. He would see to it.

"Are you sure that you're ready to leave this all behind?" he asked, straightening his linen suit.

He stood beside her taller and more hauntingly beautiful than ever. His blonde hair brandished streaks of new grey. His eyes wore lines beside them where talons of life had clawed at his face in the middle of sleepless nights. But his heart was warm and content. The love he now possessed radiated past the physical and transformed him into something one could only admire.

"Everyone already thinks that I'm dead thanks to Cory and a broke coroner," Royal said as their bodyguards escorted them. "I might as well start a new life."

He stole a look at his wife. Strong. Beautiful. Resilient. She had stood by him until her end. She had endured the sins of his life with more dignity than even he could, and she had done so at her expense with no blame.

I owe you everything, he thought to himself. It was a recurring though lately. His existence was no longer complete without her.

He grabbed her hand and led her to their private jet.

This was the end of their stories apart and the beginning of their one life together. God only knew what was in store.

Dmitry had been by Royal's side the entire time of her recovery. Every time that she woke, he was there to take care of her – feed her, bathe her, dress her, read to her. Every need had been met. Every promise kept. He did so with little to no sleep. He barely ate. He never stopped worrying.

He paid the coroner, doctors, lawyers, police and the local judges millions to stay out of jail and out of court – to keep his secret of Royal's survival.

All that he cared for was her health. It had been his dedication that kept her and his blooming daughter alive.

And it had been New York and Moscow that had come in to help the transition go smoothly. He had their blessings and therefore their protection. Men came in droves from across the world. They replenished the ranks and worked faithfully under the Medlov Family's newest boss.

Upon her recovery, Dmitry and Royal were married in their home with only Cory and Anatoly to witness a quaint, private ceremony. She could never again call her adopted family or see Renée, but the trade was worth it. She wished them all well.

Royal had known no pain after that horrible night with Ivan and no greater pleasure than being married to a man who seemed to live to provide her complete happiness.

For weeks after Ivan's attack, Royal had been displaced. The transfusions, the pain pills and the nightmares had all overwhelmed her.

For weeks, she could feel Ivan's large hands on her body, his tongue in her mouth, his scent on her skin. She remembered the thrust of his hips and the cut of his blade. But with her healing, resolve had come. Ivan's death had been retribution for his crimes against her.

Royal looked up just in time to see Dmitry lean over and kiss her lips softly.

"Let's get the hell out of here, Mrs. Medlov."

She and her entourage boarded and relaxed as the stewardess seated them and prepared the passengers for takeoff.

Quietly, Dmitry sent Anatoly a text. It simply read, "From a father to a son, thank you."

Anatoly smiled as he read it. He sped through the streets of Memphis in his father's old Mercedes-Benz with a new lease on life and a new woman in the passenger seat.

"Good Luck, Papa," he texted back. "I hope that you enjoy your new boring life cooking borscht and chasing brats."

Dmitry smiled and deleted the text.

"Everything okay, baby?" Royal asked, touching his arm.

"Everything is perfect, sweetheart," he said, grabbing the champagne off the tray.

Chapter 1

Royal screamed a blood curdling cry as Ivan held her down. His large hands were strategically placed on her naked, wounded body. Viciously, he choked her with one hand and fondled her with the other.

Spit spilled out of the side of her mouth onto his tattooed hands, and she could smell old cigarette residue on his rigid fingers.

She gasped for breath and tried to fight him, but he ignored her feeble attempts and violently snatched her legs open, scratching her inner thigh with his jagged nails.

His cold blue eyes stared directly into her own as he penetrated her. There was a look of complete satisfaction on his face as he did.

Exhausted and defeated, she turned her head to see the sharp, gleaming Glock knife beside her on the bed. The blade was so sharp until it snagged the comforter with its serrated edge due only to the friction. She swallowed hard as she looked at it, posing as a reminder to her of what he would do if she were not completely obedient.

Quickly, she said a prayer, mumbling the words under her breath as her body involuntarily pushed against the bed under his long muscular frame. He groaned and licked her bloody face.

The polarized sexual experiences stung through her as much as the pain. Dmitry loved her. Ivan loathed her. She had given her all to Dmitry. She had given nothing to Ivan, yet he took everything. Dmitry had been gentle and loving always every time that he touched her. Ivan's angry thrusts seemed to be for the purpose of impalement with deep and painful stabbings.

Pulling her face toward him, he forced her to open her mouth. His tongue slid into hers, fleshy and wet. She tried to bit his tongue but felt the knife against her throat as he threatened.

"Kiss me back like good girl," he ordered.

Cringing, she screamed out as his monstrous grip loosened around her bruised neck just enough for her to breathe. She was forced to kiss him, forced to taste him. Tears flowed freely down her face onto their skin. He wrapped his arms around her back and pulled her into his greedy erection.

"Damn, Royal," he said, hissing hot breath on her skin. "I wish Dmitry could see what I am doing to you. Not just because it would kill him." He grunted and shifted deeper. "But also because maybe he could finally see how it is done."

Screaming frantically, Royal sat up in her king-sized bed and realized that she was having yet another nightmare about Dmitry's dead brother, Ivan Medlov. Damn him. Damn him to a fiery hell, he had been dead three years now, and yet he frequently visited her in the same taunting ways.

She wiped the sweat from her forehead and ran her fingers over her neck. Her heartbeat raced against her hand. Panting, she closed her eyes and cringed as she felt the old knife mark from his blade. It had left a horrible scar that would always cause questions if she didn't cover it. However, vanity was the last issue she had. She was grateful for the scar, only because her healed wound meant that she had survived.

Pulling the many of layers of thick, plush crimson cover from her legs, she crawled out of bed and went to her bathroom. Hitting the lights, she tiptoed across the cold ceramic tile over to the sink and turned on the faucet. The sound of water filled the room, interrupting thoughts of her ghost. She ran her hands through the cold stream and washed her burning cheeks. The water soothed her soiled thoughts, cleaned her sweaty skin.

"Are you alright?" a deep voice asked behind her.

She looked up startled and saw her husband, Dmitry, standing in the oversized arched doorway. His blue eyes pierced through her, a frown darkened his fair, beautiful features.

Royal sighed. "I had another bad dream," she rolled her eyes. "I'll be fine. Where were you, anyway?" Stilling her shaking hands, she turned towards him and leaned against the vanity.

"Anya woke up and came to sleep with us. I know that you've been trying to get her to stay in her room all night, so I took her back to bed."

Turning away from him, she reached into the medicine cabinet.

"Was it Ivan again? The nightmare?" Dmitry asked softly, his baritone voice pained.

"Who else would it be?" she asked irritated.

Towering over her in on a pair of silk pajama bottoms, he walked up behind her. His bare, clean shaven chest hovered above her. Tanned to a golden bronze and covered in old world tattoos, it pulsated with concrete muscles that came from too much time in the gym and not enough time in his own bed.

Dmitry watched her fumble with the medicine bottle and finally drop two pills into her hand. Royal had been on valium for over two years. At first, it had helped her to deal with the postpartum depression after Anya was born. Then, it helped with the depression that had come after her therapy started to get over the rape. Now, it was just because. Plus, it didn't help that he owned the pharmaceutical company that produced her legal heroine; she had it sent to their home by the bulk.

Running his large hands down her sweaty back, he tried to soothe her.

"Come now, I put you back to bed," his Russian accent cut through the silence.

"I don't want to go back to bed," she snapped. Tears ran down her face. She wiped them quickly. "I want it to stop. Can you pay someone to make *that* happen?" She watched his face. "No? I didn't think so. Just leave me alone, alright. Like I said, I'll be fine."

Dmitry's guilt consumed him again for the millionth time as he watched her swallow the hand full of pills and dip her head to the faucet to drink the running water. Her long black hair fell over the sink and into the water. She ignored it, letting it whip against her gown leaving water marks as she stood back up.

"I wish there was something I could do," his voice sounded desperate.

"Just leave me alone." She held on to the sides of the water basin and looked down.

Besides the fact that she had a screeching headache and if she had to look up nearly two feet to eye him she would probably pass out, she

also did not want him to see her cry anymore.
She was tired of the constant pity and the constant reminder of what had happened to her. She
wanted desperately for it to all go away.

"Are you sure?" he asked, hoping she
wouldn't send him away.

"Yes," she hissed.

"Alright. Goodnight." He let his hand trail
off of her body.

Turning away with a defeated sigh, he left her
in the bathroom and wondered back down the
long corridor to his daughter's room.

Opening the door slowly, he looked on as
Anya slept peacefully in her twin canopy bed. He
went into the bedroom, closed the door behind
him and lay on the floor beside her bed.

Taking one of her over-sized teddy bears
from the corner, he stuck it under his head and
looked up at the painted ceiling, glowing under
pink night lights. Suddenly, there was a knock on
the door.

"Come in," he said curiously, hoping it was
Royal. He sat up.

"Master Medlov, I heard screaming. Is everything alright?" the muscular butler asked with
loaded guns in the holsters under his large arms.

"*Da Da.* We're fine, Stepan," Dmitry lay back
down. "Royal was just having another nightmare."

"Yes, sir," Stepan closed the door.

In the darkness of his daughter's room, Dmitry allowed his thoughts to consume him. Royal had been a real handful over the last six months, but she had been stricken with spells of depression since Anya's birth three years ago.

His beautiful daughter had been both a blessing and a curse at ten pounds of natural birth. Understandably, Royal had passed out only minutes after seeing her baby, a black-haired, blue-eyed doll that looked like the spitting image of his brother, Ivan.

At first sight, Dmitry had been taken back by Anya's striking beauty, but Royal had been stunned by her resemblance to the devil she had known.

Post-partum had immediately set in with Royal refusing to breast feed and spending days at a time locked in her room. Finally, the doctors were called. Dr. Finlen suggested therapy after he was told of the rape, along with time to heal the wounds and valium for the edge.

Overall, the remedy had helped, but the days that it didn't were nearly unbearable. She would have sweaty fits in her sleep and scream his brother's name in a horrible, heart-stopping cry that would send Dmitry running for her whenever he heard it.

It was like Ivan would come to rape her again and again, every time that she dared close her eyes.   This led to Royal spending many nights awake, staring blankly into the television or tossing and turning in the bed, which led to dark circles under her eyes and constant irritability.

However torturous the nightmares of Ivan were, they had not been the only thing to torment their rocky marriage. The two also hadn't been intimate in many months. The last time had been horrible for both of them.

Unknowing of the wretched words that his brother had said to her during *the assault*, Dmitry had whispered something that sent Royal into a frenzy.   Beating his chest and crying, she had begged him to stop, to *get it out* of her. He did so immediately, withdrawing ashamed and alarmed.

Like a crazed woman, Royal jumped up and literally ran out of the room, locking herself in the bathroom, where she spent the remainder of the night. He had slept on the floor beside the door that night, hoping that she might come out and talk to him. She did not.

Since that horrible event, Dmitry had barely slept in their bedroom. While her passion for him had fizzled into something repugnant, he still desired every inch of her.

To keep himself from being tempted and to continue to be cognizant of Royal's fragile state, he normally stayed in his son's bedroom when Anatoly wasn't visiting or in one of the guest bedrooms on the second level of the chateau.

He tried to never be too far from his wife that he could not be there if she needed him, but never too close – because he knew that she found him unbearable.

For the most part, he roamed the hallways at night, bored out of his mind, working out in his gym, reading volumes of classic works, and most of all waiting for a call from his son about news of the Vory.

To add insult to his injured ego, Royal also never showed him affection out of the bedroom. She was still a very gracious woman, reminding herself to always play the kind, courteous wife, but when he looked very closely, he could see the icy, angry and potentially violent woman that she had come to be.

In response to her depression, Dmitry had doubled her gifts, flying diamonds and furs in by the bus loads, just to see them pile up in her dressing rooms unopened and unworn. He had flown their family around the world on trips to exotic locales, but Royal had spent the entire time in her room, curled up in bed, crying and shaking or drugged and drinking.

When he tried to make love to her, she fled. If he saw her naked, she covered herself. The sexual frustration had nearly driven him mad. He had gone to confession only weeks ago to beg God for his forgiveness for his desire at times to take from her what was rightfully his. He had not, of course, taken it. He would never hurt her. And he had not been unfaithful. How could he?

His only desire was to be with his beautiful young wife. Even in her callous nature, she had only gotten more beautiful and refined in age. Her rich, dark caramel skin, her wide cat-like eyes, her inky mane of curly black hair with untimely streaks of grey and her voluptuous body were all exotically combined to make him livid with lust. And in a way, her razor sharp tongue provided him with a sense of humility that only she could bring.

But how he wished that the peak of her young womanhood could be spent happy and in love with him. Only, Royal was not in love. She preferred to be alone, wasting away in her bed-room with valium and scotch while her child and her husband suffered.

"Daddy, can I get in the floor with you?" Anya asked, leaning over the side of her bed. The little soft voice sounded like bells jingling.

"Of course, Angel," he said, pulling her down from her bed onto his chest.

With a doll in her hand, the small girl nestled her head down on his chest to listen to his massive heartbeat and closed her eyes.

There was an unspoken and spoken love between the two. Father and Daughter. Even with the drama of a broken home, he sheltered her and gave her materialistically and emotionally all that he could in the world.

However, unlike most children who would have spoiled because of the attention, Anya was not. She was wise for her age with a cool disposition that made most people nervous when they met her.

Kissing the crown of her head, Dmitry wrapped his arms around his daughter and sighed. At least he had her.

***

Morning came early for Royal. She was met by a door knock and her devoted young maid, who brought in her breakfast and set it on the nightstand beside her.

The French woman greeted her mistress only to receive a groan in response but that was typical. Dutifully, she then went to the large windows to pull the drapes open to receive the foggy, half-sunny day and raised the mechanical blinds that unveiled the breathtaking view of acres and acres of unspoiled, mountainous green land.

Wrapped in sweat-stained sheets, Royal rose from her slumber in a daze. Vision blurred and hair wild, she rested her feet on the side of the bed and stared blankly at the oversized fireplace in front of her.

If she had any balls at all, she would simply jump into the large fire pit and meet her miserable end, but she didn't have balls at all so she settled for grabbing the remote and turning on the flat screen hoisted above the mantle.

"Madame, would you like for me to run your bath?" the young maid asked in a thick French accent, picking up dirty clothes off the bedroom floor.

"No," Royal said absently. "And put those clothes back. I'll clean up my own mess."

"Yes, Madame," she said, dropping the clothes. "Is there anything else I can do for you this morning?"

Royal sighed. "Where's my daughter?" She scratched her head.

"Having breakfast downstairs with Master Medlov."

"Of course, she is," Royal stood up. "Tell me, Brigitte, how's your mom these days?"

"I'm afraid that she is not doing so well, Madame."

"The treatments didn't help, huh?"

"No, not enough to make it go away," the woman lamented.

"You have…bags under your eyes," Royal observed lazily. "You look like shit." She yawned and stretched.

"Forgive my presentation, Madame. I have acquired another job at night to help with the bills. Keeping it all together has been most difficult."

"Another job?" Royal shook her head. "Does Dmitry not pay you enough?"

"It's the best paying job I've ever had, Madame. I am very grateful for your family and your gracious…"

"Save it. Dmitry could pay you more. He knows your situation," Royal grabbed her bottle of valium by the bed. "But I'm afraid you'd have to give him something in return." She smirked. "You're a pretty girl, so it's probably something you don't even have anymore."

"Excuse me, Mistress Medlov?"

"Nothing. I'm being hateful, Brigitte. Do you know this term, *hateful?*"

"Yes."

"Well, you'll have to excuse me for it." Dropping pills in her hand, she put them in her mouth quickly and drank the last of the scotch sitting in the glass by her nightstand. "You didn't see that," she snapped at Brigitte. "I know

Dmitry will ask you questions as soon as you leave out of here. He always does. Makes you spy for him." She cut her eyes at the woman.

"He is just concerned," Brigitte explained.

"*Concerned* my overpriced ass. He's just bored."

Royal walked into her large, adjoining dressing room with her long satin gown trailing behind her. Quickly, she turned on the lights and sat down at her hand-carved wooden vanity. Pulling out a small drawer, she flipped open the velvet Velcro box and pulled out a new necklace from Tiffany's that Dmitry had recently purchased for her.

"Money is so hard to come by these days," she said, running her finger over the diamonds. "Had it not been for my cursed womb, I might be cleaning rooms just like you. Don't ever be ashamed of what you do. It's a respectable job."

"Yes, Madame," the maid said, standing up straighter.

Brigitte walked curiously to the door opening and waited with her hands clasped together in front of her.

Mistress Medlov was a strange woman. Her eyes were cold, her stare blank, her words laced with vicious meaning. One never knew what to expect from her. She was mostly tongue and cheek with all her statements, but if one were to look very, very carefully, they could see that once she had to have been a good woman. Why else would a man as gracious as Master Medlov have married her, besides her stunning beauty and her exotic dark features?

In Prague, her beauty stuck out everywhere that she went. She was the *la belle femme de couleur.*

The mistress dressed in very expensive clothes and jewelry and stomped around town chauffeured in the most luxurious cars. She had a strange American accent. *Southern* is what Dmitry had once called it. And all of the officials, politicians and businessmen who visited the Medlov chateau, swooned over her, even though she treated them callously also.

But there was something else. All the help talked about it. Royal had presence, not stage presence, a dark, mischievous presence like she was capable of just about anything. She was far from helpless, very quick and too observant. Some said she was even more dangerous than Master Medlov.

She stared at the back of her lady's wild hair now as Royal fumbled around, probably looking for more valium.

"*Oui*, it is very hard for everyone, but…" she finally continued the conversation, realizing that she had lost herself for a moment in thought.

"Not everyone," Royal corrected. A smile curved her pensive lips. Standing up with the necklace, she walked over to the Brigitte and grabbed her hand. "You are lucky to have a mother to care for, whether she is dying of cancer or not. You'll always have good memories. Treasure them."

"*Oui*," the maid agreed. "I am very blessed."

"Take this home with you today. Pawn it and pay for whatever your mother needs. Quit your other job and go home to spend more time with her before she's dead, because she will die. If the treatments aren't working, there's not a damned thing that you can do about it. Meanwhile, I'll talk to your gracious boss, Dmitry, about giving you a *meaningful* raise."

"But Madame…I can't. This necklace costs more than I make in a year."

Royal gripped the woman's hand firmly. "Then be smart, Briggy. Don't tell anyone that I've given it to you."

Brigitte fought tears. She was moved by the icy woman's kind gesture. Mistress Medlov was like that though. Completely unreadable.

"If you have a problem at the local jeweler's, call me. No one will believe that you didn't steal it," Royal looked away from Brigitte, who wiped her tears quickly.

"*Merci*," the woman said softly.

"Don't mention it," Royal said curtly.

Like wind chimes on a gusty spring afternoon, Anya's voice carried as she called for her mother. Royal looked away from Brigitte to her beautiful daughter wide-eyed and smiling from ear to ear as she came running as fast as she could through the bedroom doors. Suddenly, Royal lit up.

"Ahh, there she is."

Royal caught her in her arms and picked her up to hold her close to her bosom. Rubbing through her long, black silky hair, she kissed her daughter's forehead and sighed.

"Mommy, what are you doing?"

"Nothing, baby. What are you up to?"

"I had breakfast with Daddy."

"You slept in your room last night. I'm very proud of you, princess."

"I cheated, Mommy. Daddy slept with me."

Royal smiled and nodded to Brigitte to leave her alone to spend time with her one and only purpose, Anya.

"Anatoly is here," Anya tattled. "He and Daddy are downstairs in the...the...study. They told me I had to leave."

"Really," Royal said curiously. "What were they talking about? Can you remember?" She pulled the girl closer.

"Anatoly said that he had a problem that only Daddy could fix."

"Did he?" Royal placed her daughter on the disheveled bed. "And what did Daddy say?"

"He said I had to run along. Then he closed the big doors and locked me out." Anya pouted. "Why did he lock me out, Mommy?"

"Because he's up to something, baby," Royal took off her nightgown and threw it on the bed. She was going to get down to the bottom of this right now.

"Let mommy get dressed, and I'll come downstairs with you, so we can say hello to your long lost brother."

Chapter 2

Immaculately dressed, Royal arrived downstairs an hour later to have her breakfast in the great room with her bodyguard Davyd, while Anya played outside on the patio with her puppy.

The weather had taken a turn for the worse. Where the sun peaked out of the clouds only a half an hour before, now thick dark clouds rolled through the green plush countryside, promising rain and dreariness for the remainder of the day.

Dmitry's decision to take her half way across the world to a place that she had never seen had turned out to be a bad idea in her opinion. However, considering that to the only world that she had ever known, she was dead, her options were limited.

Royal sipped her coffee slowly and stared at the newspaper. Her thoughts multiplied by the second. What was that husband of hers up to?

Davyd watched Royal carefully as he sipped his own coffee and monitored Anya as she played. Royal was more than not herself today. Something else was going on. He put down his coffee and sighed. His blue eyes locked on her. How long would it take for her to tell him? He was her confidant, more so even than Dmitry. Being that, it frustrated him when she didn't just say what was on her mind, when she made him figure it out.

"Do I have to ask?" he uttered finally under his breath to make sure that no one would hear him.

"Anatoly is here," Royal said, smacking her lips together. "You know what that means."

"He wants to see his family," Davyd looked over at Anya. "You know how crazy he is about his little sister."

"Uh huh," Royal scoffed. "His little princess overheard him say that he needed his father's help."

"You're always jumping to conclusions."

"We'll see, won't we?"

"You should be focused on other things, Royal. Today, Anya's new teacher arrives. Dmitry said that she came highly recommended. Still, she'll be living in your home and helping rear your child. And that is much more important than what Anatoly wants with his own father."

"Mind your tongue, old man. I know my priorities."

"Mind your tongue and your attitude, *Mistress Medlov*. Sometimes, I think that you were born on wrong side of bed. And don't think that I don't know you slipped drink before coming downstairs. I can smell it underneath all that perfume."

Royal cut her eyes at him but did not respond. Davyd had become something of a vicar to her.

After the attack, he had been assigned to Royal day-in and day-out. And because of their time together, they had become family. She regarded his knowledge of the Vory, which he secretly shared with her, his familiarity with Prague and his experience with Dmitry with extreme reverence. He was like the father that she had never had at thirty-two years her elder and because of this allowed him to freely share his opinions.

Plus, she didn't want him to know that his scathing remark had humbled her…for the moment.

"I see that you are finally awake," Dmitry said, walking into the room with his son closely following. "Did you get some sleep?"

"As much as to be expected," she said, picking her coffee cup back up and holding it close to her lips. She felt Davyd's foot kick her. "I slept reasonably well, dear," she retracted.

"Good." Leaning over, Dmitry kissed her head. "Where's Anya?"

"Right outside playing with her puppy."

"So she liked it?" Anatoly asked. He had given her a chocolate lab for her birthday only a few weeks ago. He stood in the corner by the window with his arms crossed looking out at Anya.

"She loves it," Royal smiled. "What brings you back to Prague so quickly? Is there trouble in paradise, Anatoly?"

Anatoly looked up at Dmitry and raised his brow. "Can't I just come and visit?" There was an incredibly mischievous smile on his face.

"You don't *just* do anything," Royal said quickly. She eyed Dmitry as he sat down across from her. "So, what is going on?' Her voice lowered. Something deep in her stomach tugged at her –something was wrong.

"If you must know, Anatoly is thinking of selling Dmitry's Closet. It's not bringing in nearly the revenue it did before," Dmitry responded, picking up the discarded newspaper.

Davyd sat quietly observing the two. He hoped that Royal would behave.

"Are the people of Memphis no longer fascinated with the tourist attraction that it's come to be?" Royal huffed sarcastically. "Oh well. It couldn't last forever." She didn't lead on to her thinking more was involved.

"You know, you should spend more time down at your *new* shop," Dmitry suggested to

Royal. "It will give you something to do, maybe make you happier."

"And what makes you think that I'm not happy?" she bit out in a growl.

Anatoly laughed, and then turned away from the troubled couple. Even Davyd almost laughed. Royal was like a constant thorn in her husband's side, but still Dmitry did not waiver in his attention to her.

Anatoly found the cat and mouse game boring and overly dramatic. However, if his father was happy in his torture, then so was he.

Dmitry sighed and changed the subject. "The teacher will be here today. Very soon in fact," he looked down at his Rolex. "I was hoping since you did not take part in interview process that you would *at least* talk to her today, lay out ground rules of house and give her instruction as to what you want her to do with Anya."

"That's simple. I want her to go back to where she came from. I can teach my own daughter. I don't need some *nanny* coming in here like I'm incompetent."

"She's only here to help. And no one thinks that you're incompetent. You said yourself you wanted more time to focus on you, more time to focus on the boutique...."

"She's not welcome here as far as I'm concerned. But since you have already sent for her,

I'll find something for her to do. After I teach Anya myself then she can tutor her as a follow up....or whatever." She rolled her eyes again, knowing that the entire room was now focused on her. Trying to justify her position, she tried to stop her whining. "This is just stupid. I mean, just because everyone else has a teacher doesn't mean we have to. We're not like everyone else," she reminded them all.

The butler, Stepan, walked into the great room and interrupted the would-be argument.

Dmitry took his eyes off his visibly disturbed wife and looked up at him. He waved the butler to come closer.

"Ms. Victoria Jackson has arrived, sir. Should I have her come in here, or would you like to talk with her in the family room?"

"The family room," Royal interjected. She huffed. Why didn't anyone understand that she didn't want some woman in her home? Who in their right mind would want that?

"Yes, ma'am," Stepan turned and walked out.

"*Beeeeehave*, Royal," Dmitry ordered. He clinched his jaw.

"You behave," she hissed.

Cutting his eyes at her, he stood up from the table and went to the large glass double doors. He didn't want to admit it, but suddenly he felt the same apprehension as his ever-unhappy wife.

Calling for Anya, he finally shut out his concern as his little girl scurried in with her puppy.

"The dog doesn't come inside," Royal ordered. "I've told you that a thousand times." Her tongue was sharp.

"Yes, mama," Anya pushed her puppy out of the door quickly. "Go on, Bubbles."

"Is that what you named him?" Anatoly asked her as he picked her up to carry her to the family room.

"Yes, his name is *Mr.* Bubbles, because Mommy said everyone has to have a title." Anya wrapped her small arms around her brother and kissed his face.

"She called one of the gardeners by his first name the other day. And I was explaining to her that just because he works for us doesn't mean that he doesn't deserve respect. That is why we use titles."

No one could deny Royal's logic or how kind she was to everyone *outside* of the family at the chateau.

"Where are you going?" Royal asked Anatoly as he followed Dmitry.

"With you," he chuckled. "I wouldn't miss this for the world."

"You're not helping," Dmitry warned Anatoly without looking back as he slipped on his suit jacket.

Neither are you, Anatoly thought to himself. Was he the only one who thought that this was a bad idea?

***

As her mystery guest waited, Royal stormed through the family room's large oak double doors with her entourage of Dmitry, Anatoly, Anya and Davyd in tow.

Dressed to kill in a black knee-length leather skirt that narrowed her bow hips, a wide black leather belt that accentuated her voluptuous curves, black leather boots that stopped mid-calf and gave her several inches of height, and black cashmere turtleneck that only enhanced her large breasts, Royal stopped at the top of the short stairs that led down the main level of the room to see a woman standing in the middle of the floor.

The tall teacher stopped and turned, transfixed by the stately mistress of the house. Although Dmitry had previously warned that his wife was a bit stoic in the interview, his explanation had not done justice to the perfect beauty, who seemed at first sight to be unwelcoming.

Dmitry also had not mentioned that his wife was black or at least mixed. From first sight, Mistress Medlov's features were so exotic it was hard to pinpoint exactly what she was, but there was evident melanin that suggested African heritage, and her body was definitely sister-like with busty curves and a mean diva walk.

"Ahh, you must be Victoria," Royal said with a sly grin. She knew Dmitry was watching her, praying for her not to misbehave and send this wench flying out of the front door. It was a tall order, but she tried hard to comply.

"Yes, ma'am. You must be Mistress Medlov," the woman spoke in an American English accent.

"I am."

Anatoly smirked. That wasn't all that Royal was, but he would let the poor woman find out on her own.

"You sound American."

Royal started down the steps as her clan dispersed around the room to various vantage points to watch the event unfold without their views being obstructed.

"I am. I'm from…" Victoria paused and looked around the elegantly designed room. "I'm from D.C. by way of the Dominican Republic. My family moved to the states when I was a baby."

Royal walked up to her and offered her well manicured, diamond drenched hand. She shook her hand firmly, looking her up and down, inspecting the new help. "I've never been to either place, but I've heard tons about them."

"They are very diverse places," Victoria answered, releasing her hand. "What city are you from?"

Royal raised her brow. "All over. But enough about me. This is my family. You already know my husband Dmitry, who went through the labor of hiring you. That is my daughter, *your pupil*, Anya." She turned and pointed in the opposite direction at the corner bar. "His son, Anatoly. And my bodyguard, Davyd."

"Nice to meet you all," Victoria said with a nod of her head. Her eyes lingered toward the blue prisms of Anatoly's eyes as he too sized her up. He gave a sly nod and turned back around in his seat away from the drama and the young stranger.

Victoria Jackson was a tall, dark and strikingly beautiful woman. Her perfectly toned, milk chocolate skin gave contrast to the designer winter white wool suit cut to fit her long slender body and brought out her bright brown eyes.

She radiated style and elegance with perfectly erect posture and an apparent social grace that Royal chalked up to her being from a good family and having a good education, which had been two of Dmitry's prerequisites for this position.

"We're very happy to have you here," Dmitry said, walking up to Victoria and Royal with Anya. He sensed the need to interject in the conversation before it turned sour. He could see that his wife was trying to be gracious but could feel her anxiety from across the room.

"Thank you, Mr. Medlov," Victoria said, shaking his hand.

He was a breath of fresh air in the room. His smile calmed her. Unable to keep her attention from the beautiful little girl, she looked down at Anya.

"You're a very gorgeous little girl. I can't wait for us to begin our classes tomorrow."

"Daddy said that you were going to teach me a lot of new things," Anya smiled, holding on to her father's trousers. "But Mommy said you're just one more person to irritate her."

"Anya," Dmitry corrected as he looked down at Royal, who only smirked.

"It's okay," Victoria smiled but noted the concern.

Anatoly laughed and swirled his ice around in his water. He could always count on Anya to liven things up a little.

"Don't scold her, Dmitry. I *did* say it," Royal countered, taking up for her daughter. "But let's just hope that that isn't the case." She smiled at Victoria.

"I'll do my best, Mrs. Medlov," Victoria said courteously.

"Good, now if you come with me, I'm going to escort you to your new living quarters, make sure that you get everything that you need to be comfortable and leave you for the rest of the day on your own," she turned and waved at Stepan to get Victoria's luggage. She couldn't wait to get this woman as far away from her family as possible. There was just something about her that she did not like.

"Well, I was hoping that she could join us for dinner tonight, since it is her first night here," Dmitry added.

Even Anatoly looked over with a cocked brow. *Was he crazy?* He and Davyd made eye contact.

Royal stopped. *Now*, he was pushing it. "Oh. Well, okay. Then, we'll call for you around dinner time. It's normally around six." Her smile was half crooked. The patience she had mustered was now starting to wear thin and not with the woman but also with Dmitry.

"Yes, ma'am. I'll be here." Victoria sensed Royal's resistance to the imposition but chose not to decline his offer. After all, her checks were written by Mr. Medlov, not his stuck up wife.

"Can I go with you, Mommy?" Anya asked, reaching for Royal's hand.

"Yeah, baby." Royal picked her up and planted her comfortably on her left hip while giving Dmitry a very dirty look.

Together, the three women left the room with Royal leading quietly, fighting the sudden desire to crawl up the side of her husband's body and rip his eyeballs from their sockets.

***

As the doors closed behind them, there was a collective sigh among the men. Dmitry turned with a clever smile and went to the bar, where Anatoly and Davyd sat, to pour himself a drink.

"That didn't go *so* badly," he said, raising his glass at the men.

"It went worse," Anatoly answered. "You've just started World War three under your own roof and with no exit strategy."

"How? By providing more structure for Anya? Please," Dmitry scoffed.

"Did you have to pick a black woman?" Anatoly asked. He shook his head. "Royal is going to kill you both."

"I don't want anything to do with Ms. Jackson. She's here for Anya." He sipped his drink and looked over at Davyd. "Well, weigh in. I know you want to."

"It's not my place," Davyd said quickly.

"Then make it your place," Dmitry urged.

"She's too...beautiful, Dmitry," Davyd explained. "Royal will feel she's in competition. And you don't want *that* woman any more combative. She's already handful." Davyd would not betray Royal's trust and tell Dmitry that his wife's self-esteem could not take such a hard blow.

"I'm not stupid. I know Victoria is beautiful, but she's also most qualified. Plus, I know her family. Her father owes me big favors, and he's still on my payroll."

"I give it one month," Anatoly smirked.

"I give it one week," Davyd bet against him.

"She's been commissioned for *one year*, until Anya starts pre-school at the academy. This will help her have the edge she needs for school. Plus, Victoria went to Brown. She's a world traveler, and she plans to work for a reputable school for girls abroad soon. Learning how to understand families from inside helps her develop skills."

"You don't have to sell us, papa," Anatoly grabbed the bottle of vodka. "I will be on plane out of here soon. You, on the other hand, will still be here with the two of them."

Davyd chuckled.

"Maybe this will help Royal," Dmitry said seriously. "She needs something to focus on. Having Victoria here might give her a chance to find out what that is."

"As your wife puts it often, *we'll see*," Davyd said, getting up. "I better go and get car ready to take Royal to her shop."

"She's going to work today?" Dmitry was shocked.

"Da, Da. She told me yesterday that she wanted to go and check on everything today."

"See," Dmitry smiled. "Progress already."

***

The Medlov chateau was far too luxurious for words.   Victoria walked quietly behind Mrs. Medlov and her curious daughter, who eyed her the entire time as she gawked at the endless limestone staircases, the marble posts, the incredible lighting, the extravagant tapestry, the endless hallways, the statues, the priceless rugs, the one-of-a-kind art, artifacts, the vases, the lighting... it was all too much.

"Mommy said *marvel not*," Anya said, finally as she ran her hand down Royal's shoulder.

"Excuse me?" Victoria asked quietly.

"You aren't supposed to marvel at things," Anya said in a matter-of-fact tone.

"Now, now," Royal admonished. "She's not a child like you. She doesn't need *your* help or *my* preaching."

"No, ma'am. That's not what I meant," Victoria was amazed. "It's the fact that she not only knew what I was doing but that she could articulate such a thing."

"Yes, well, Anya's special," Royal said stopping at a large door. Taking a key out of her pocket, she unlocked the door and led Victoria inside.

"Dmitry made sure that you had a nice room," Royal said absently. Seeing Victoria's face light up brought back old memories of when Dmitry had first given her an apartment. She looked away as she tried to hide her jealousy.

"Mrs. Medlov, this is absolutely…."

"I know," Royal interrupted. "Let's go through the rules this one time."

Victoria stopped *marveling* as Anya had put it and focused. "Alright."

"All of the staff lives here on the third floor. No one outside of Stepan and Davyd are allowed on the second floor. That's where the family lives. You can bypass the second floor by going back down the same flight of stairs that I just brought you up. I'll make sure Anya is downstairs every morning by eight. She can start classes at nine, after breakfast."

"Yes, Mistress."

"I'll handle your pay. I'll handle any problems that you have. And I'll handle Anya. I don't want you to make yourself available to anyone in the house. No relationships with the other staff.

No interaction with my step son. Absolutely, no interaction with my husband. Are we clear?" Her voice hardened.

"Yes, Mistress. We are clear."

"Good, these instructions are for your own good. I can't be responsible for what might happen if you don't listen." Royal couldn't come right out and tell the woman that they were a mafia family, but she could at least warn her, *even if she didn't like her.* It was the most that she could do, but if the woman was obedient, it would be enough.

"Yes, Mistress."

"Now, I'll have Stepan go out and get what- ever you need to make this room more comfort- able for you. You have your own phone, com- puter and laptop in your study, which is the next room over. You also have an entertainment center with a large television, DVD player and movies. It gets…lonely out here. So you'll need this. *Trust me.*"

"Thank you."

Royal took Anya's hand and started to walk out of the door. She stopped suddenly and turned around. "Oh, and more thing, Victoria. Dinner is optional after tonight. You don't have to feel obligated to dine with us. We have a great cook on staff, who stays two doors down from you. All you have to do is call down to the kitchen, and he'll bring you almost anything that you can imagine up to your quarters."

"I understand," Victoria said, bowing her head once more.

As Royal closed the door behind her and left with Anya, Victoria rolled her eyes and kicked off her shoes. What a bitch! She hadn't been there ten minutes and already the woman was going through her *don't-mess-with-my-man* routine.

Victoria could tell at first sight that she didn't like Mistress Medlov, but she knew that the woman felt the same way about her.

However, she could understand why. With a husband as fine as Dmitry, she would be tripping too, especially since he liked sisters. Plus, his son, Anatoly, was a sexy thing too. She caught him checking her out on the slick side. Then, Davyd was like an old sexy grandpa with the damned guns visible for everyone to see. This family was off the chain.

Her dad had told her to tread carefully here and do this favor for Mr. Medlov, a friend of the family that she had never met or heard of before he called. It was just like her father to know some of the shadiest people in the world. Lobbying for gun rights had its perks, she guessed.

She smiled to herself. There wasn't much to complain about here. She was going to make 150,000 Euros to work for *Mistress Hardass* for one year. She got most weekends off; she got most holidays off; and she'd fine something or someone to keep her busy when she wasn't working. Good thing that she already had *someone* in mind.

Chapter 3

Dmitry pushed through his last set of skull crushers as he thought about Royal. She'd been out in the courtyard all day with the gardeners giving them direction on how she wanted the landscaping done for spring, which was most unlike her.

However, since Victoria had come to the chateau over two weeks ago, it seemed that his wife was determined to keep busy and stay even farther away from him than before.

Her distance only made things worse between them, and he had every intention of taking the matter up with her today. But it seemed she had sensed the confrontation coming and immediately found a reason to be preoccupied the entire first half of the day.

Flat on his back with sweat glistening, he grunted as he let the bar plop loudly back in the rack and sat up. He breathed in heavily, grabbed a towel to wipe his face and looked over at the clock. He'd been in his gym for over an hour. Exhausted, he slipped on his t-shirt and headed up to his room to jump in the shower.

As he headed down the long corridor that led from his gym into the common rooms of the house, he heard his daughter giggling and laughing. Curiously, he stopped at the door of her new study room and stuck his head inside. Victoria was sitting Indian-style in the middle of the floor with a book in her hand reading, while Anya sat across from her on a pillow. They were evidently having a great time. He cleared his voice and tapped on the door.

Anya automatically looked his way then scurried to her feet and greeted him with a huge hug.

"*Daaaaddddyyyy*, where have you been?" she asked, kissing his sweaty face as he scooped her up.

"In the gym, baby," he said, whirling her around.

Victoria stood up and smoothed out her jeans. Her face lit up when she saw him. To look at the beautiful giant was a treat in itself, but to see him glistening in sweat, muscles bulging in his gym clothes made her heart skip a beat. Plus, she would have never guessed that such a refined man had so many tattoos. They made him even sexier and even harder to resist.

"Mr. Medlov," she said blushing. "We were not expecting you." She tried not to look directly at his penis, but she did steal a peak.

"Sorry to interrupt. I heard someone laughing," he explained, kissing his daughter. "And I could not resist."

"No imposition at all," Victoria walked over to the happy pair. She could not resist either. "Anya has been a wonderful student." She reached up and rubbed Anya's arm. "We're having so much fun together."

They made eye contact, and Dmitry realized that maybe he should not have intruded after all. There was a sexual energy between them that he hadn't felt since Royal dismissed him. He recognized it right away.

"I'm glad that you two are getting along. Anya seems happy and so daddy is happy," he looked at his daughter.

"We can't have you unhappy, now can we?" Victoria knew what she was doing, baiting him.

Dmitry raised his brow. Was she serious? "Well, I had better let you all get back to your lesson," he sat Anya down. Looking down at the young woman, he smiled politely. "You two have a good day." His eyes sparkled.

Her heart skipped two beats. "We were actually about to go to lunch," Victoria said anxiously. She took Anya's hand. "So we can walk with you, if you're going our way."

Dmitry instantly felt that even being around Victoria would create a problem between him and Royal, but he couldn't spend the entire year avoiding the woman when he had no intention of pursuing her.

"Will you walk with us to the great room, Daddy?" his daughter begged, pulling at his sweat pants. *"Pleeeeeease."*

"Da Da, I walk with you, angel," he said, stepping out of the way so that the two women could pass him.

As they walked down the long corridor to the great room, Anya skipped ahead of them singing while he and Victoria followed.

Pulling her hair behind her ear, Victoria smiled and sighed. "This has really been a wonderful experience, Mr. Medlov. Thank you so much for choosing me."

"Thank you for choosing us, Victoria. Anya seems really happy. And please, call me Dmitry." He slipped his hands in his pockets and tried not to look her way.

"Alright," she blushed again. Even though it was apparent that he had just worked out, his cologne floated down to her nose. She took in a deep breath and changed the subject. "I hope that Mrs. Medlov has had enjoyed me being here as well."

Dmitry smirked and looked up at the vaulted ceiling. "I'm sure she has," he said, biting his lip as he lied. "Mrs. Medlov has been under a lot of stress, so you'll have to excuse her if she's ever short with you."

"Oh, she's always really nice." Lie. "Being the overseer of a place like this is a big chore in itself, I imagine. But she does a very good job."

Victoria knew that giving his wife compliments would only make him more comfortable to be around her. And she needed him to relax in order for her plan to work. He was always so tense and alert. *Let your guard down*, she begged inwardly.

"Umm, she does work hard," Dmitry agreed. His mind was already back on his wife at just the mention of her name. "When we came to Prague, this chateau was abandoned, and we were actually living in the city in a new loft that had recently been built. But Royal wanted to move to the countryside and raise Anya out here, where things are more peaceful. So, I bought this chateau from a friend, and she immediately started to renovate it. She's been working hard in it ever since."

"Well, it's very impressive." Victoria smirked to herself. She would have never guessed *that* woman ever raised finger to do anything except give someone an order.

There was silence as they walked beside each other. Dmitry thought again of Royal and her hard work, while Victoria relished in being near him.

"What…um, if you don't mind me asking, what is Mrs. Medlov's first name?"

Dmitry looked over at her and paused. "Chloe," he said finally. "But I am sure that she would prefer Mistress Medlov."

"Oh, I sort of figured that. I just wondered. No one calls her by her first name here. I've never even really heard you say it."

Dmitry gave no explanation.

They stopped at the door of the great room, and Victoria turned and looked up at him.

"Sure you don't want to have lunch with us? We're having peanut butter and jelly," she asked, fluttering her eyebrows. She moved in a little closer but not close enough to be considered intimate. She looked at his chest, wondering what it must feel like to touch it, to touch him.

"As much as I love *peanut butter and jelly*, I better pass," he said, holding on to the towel around his neck.

"Going once, going twice…"

"I think that he said no," Royal said, walking out of the room with a tray clinched in her hands. Eyebrows spiked, she peered at the woman.

Victoria jumped, startled at her presence. The maid normally delivered lunch, but it appeared that the mistress of the house had chosen to serve her daughter today.

In a pair of dirty jeans, a grey flannel shirt and work boots, Royal walked out into the hallway and roughly passed the silver serving tray to Victoria.

"Mrs. Medlov, I thought that you were out in your garden. I would have invited you as well," Victoria said quickly.

"*Was* in the garden," Royal sneered. "I figured that I would fix you both lunch to thank you for a job well done. So, you had better go enjoy it before it gets cold," she ordered, turning her stare to Dmitry.

"Thank you, Mrs. Medlov," Victoria said, looking at Dmitry one last time. Neither Dmitry nor Mistress Medlov was paying attention to her at that point, so she quickly went inside to join Anya.

Dmitry looked his wife up and down. She was dirty from work, angry from jealousy and her nipples had hardened through her shirt. A sly grin crossed his face.

"You look great," he said, licking his lips. His eyes were hooded now, focused in on her small waist. His mouth watered.

"You look like you're up to something," she said, turning to go up to her room.

"Up to what?" he asked behind her.

"Flirting with the *help*," she bit out.

Dmitry walked behind her, following her as she swayed. "Please. What do I want with her, when I have you?"

"Don't blow smoke up my ass, Dmitry," Royal snapped.

Dmitry laughed. "I'm not blowing smoke up your ass," he said, catching up with her. He grabbed her arm and turned her around. "Wait. Slow down, now. I want to talk to you."

"About what?"

"About us."

Royal folded her arms. "What about *us*, Dmitry? What is it that I've done wrong now?" He didn't know how sensitive she was about doing wrong in his eyes. She hid it successfully with venom, but inside all she ever wanted was to please him.

"You know what I want to talk to you about." He rubbed her arms. "You're getting more and more distant. What is this about? Is it me?"

"I'm not getting distant. I've been busy." *Trying to please you*, she thought inwardly. *Look at this place. Is it not immaculate? All that I do for you…* she cut her thoughts off.

"Have you been going to therapy?" Dmitry could see anguish in her tired eyes.

"Are we going to go through that again?" she huffed. "No. I haven't been going. I don't need to go. I just need to get past it, and going and talking about it every week doesn't help."

"Have the nightmares gone away, then?"

"You know that they haven't." She had just had one the night before.

"Exactly. This is why you need to go."

Royal rolled her eyes. "I don't want to talk about this now."

"Then when?"

"I don't know. Just not right now." She threw up her hands. "I've been working all day in the dirt and with horse manure. I smell like shit…I feel like…I want to take a hot bath and rest before I go to the shop. Is that so much to ask?"

"You're going to work again today?"

"Yes. Isn't that what you wanted?"

Dmitry sighed and let her go. "We talk tonight as soon as you get home." He raised his finger to her nose, flipped it and walked away. Their footsteps echoed down the large hallway as they went in opposite directions.

Victoria listened on near the door opening and soaked up all the information that she could. So, there was a problem between the happy couple. She knew it. Smiling, she leaned against the door and popped her lips. How could any-one be distant from a man like Dmitry Medlov? And Mrs. Medlov was in therapy? Crazy bitch.

Her vice was probably alcohol. She had smelled it on her breath at least four times since she started working for them.

"What are you doing, Victoria?" Anya asked, getting up from the table.

"Nothing," Victoria said in hushed tone. She darted cross the room. "Finish eating your food and after that we can go outside and play for a while."

Chapter 4

Brigitte let out a soft moan and rubbed the blonde hair hovering over her. Kissing his lips as he rose from her breasts, she melted in his strong arms. His strokes were slow and accurate, filling her to the brim with ecstasy. As his hips retracted, she began to shiver, feeling him instantly return with full thrusts inside of her.

Gripping his back, she watched as her full breasts bounced against the magnitude of his pressure. With the flick of his thumb, he teased her aching nipples before he buried his head back to taste her.

"Master...Medlov," she moaned as the wetness of her body saturated his sheets.

"Shh," he whispered as he pulled her legs up over his shoulders. "Not too loud. We don't want anyone to hear, *eh*?" A devilish grin crossed his face. "You feel so good, Brigitte." He thrust into her again, this time holding down her hips to the mattress. "Did you miss me?"

"*Oui*," she pined. "*Oui, oui, oui.*"

"How much?" he asked with a powerful push. "This much...or this much?" Sweat ran down his muscular chest on to his carved abs.

Brigitte bit her lip and grabbed her breasts. The feeling of a familiar, powerful climax approached.

"*Ahh….ohhh…ummm,*" she whimpered as his strokes became stronger. "So much."

"That's it," he said, grunting as he picked her body up off the bed. "Let me feel it."

Her long blonde hair fell over his arm as he gripped her small waist. Rubbing his bronzed, tattooed body, she looked up at the ceiling and released. Shaking all over, she tried to cover her mouth as she screamed, hearing him chuckle in a husky tone before he grunted and came inside of her, holding her close as he did so.

They both fell back onto the bed, sweating and panting. She looked over into his blue eyes and kissed his lips. Anatoly pulled her close to him and moved her long blonde locks out of his way to see her glowing face better. They kissed softly for a minute before she laid her head back down on the pillow.

"You're still on birth control, *Da?*" he whispered into her ear.

"Yes," she said, curling under him. "Are you still faithful, my love?"

Anatoly smirked. "I'm safe. I got checked last week. Passed it with flying colors." He ran his finger down her long frame.

Brigitte closed her eyes and sighed. Having been hoping for a different answer, she was mildly disappointed to know how he still felt. They had been breaking Mistress Medlov's rules for nearly three months now. It was love at first sight for her, but she knew that Anatoly only liked her. Still, when they made love the passion was unexplainable and undeniable. She could not resist him.

"What are you thinking about?" she asked, when she recognized his silence.

"I'm still horny," he said, slipping his fingers in between her wet thighs. "I can't quite get enough."

She giggled. Anatoly was an animal.

Rolling over on her back, she looked up at him as he hovered over her, viral and carnal in all his ways. He was such a beautiful man. Dirty blonde locks, ice blue eyes, a perfectly straight nose, square jaw, perfect white teeth, a muscular tattooed frame, money, power and drive.

How she wanted him. How she wanted him to want more of her than he took. Her thoughts subsided as he entered her and her eyes closed shut. A gasp crossed her lips as he bent down to her kiss her. She ran her hands over the ripple of muscles in his back and prepared to enjoy more of him before he was off to do *whatever* he did.

Suddenly the door opened.   Anatoly pulled out and turned around.

"Shit, papa!" he said, pulling the covers over Brigitte.

Planted at the door, Dmitry stood with a pair of pants and towel in his hands and a blank look on his face.

"I didn't know you had arrived," Dmitry said in a deep Russian baritone. He did not blink or look directly at the naked woman.

"You were in gym when I got here," Anatoly explained. He wiped the sweat from his forehead and rubbed it on the comforter.

"I'll use other bedroom to get dressed. My wife is using her entire room right now and not even bathroom is available." He was more so explaining to Brigitte than Anatoly.

"She's pissed at you?" Anatoly asked.

"Of course," Dmitry smirked. "Both of you get dressed now. And you," he said, pointing at Anatoly, "Meet me in my study so we can talk."

"Alright," Anatoly said, jumping out of bed naked.

Dmitry closed and locked the door behind him.

***

After a quick shower and a change of clothes, Dmitry made his way to his study where Anatoly sat waiting for him and drinking a glass of Royal's homemade iced tea.

With a grin, Dmitry walked in and closed the doors behind him, eyeing his son curiously for an explanation of what he was doing in bed with the maid.

The sun had finally come out and shined brightly through the study's large bay windows giving a breathtaking view of the landscape.

Unable to help himself, he stopped and looked out the window, marveling at God's work and the peace of his existence. There was always calm before the storm. He looked over at his son.

Finally taking a seat behind his credenza, Dmitry shuffled through his papers then looked up and clasped his hands together.

"I would tell you to tell me everything, but I'm afraid that I don't want to know all the details, I just want to know why," he finally said as Anatoly leaned closer in his seat to the desk.

"She's beautiful, isn't she?" Anatoly raised a brow. His eyes sparkled. "She's like summertime."

Dmitry was taken aback by his son's answer but nodded. "*Da Da*, she is beautiful, but she's also Royal's pet. If she found out that you were sleeping with her maid, she might fire Brigitte just to keep her away from you. Then, I would be the only one who benefits, since she made me double your girlfriend's salary a few weeks ago."

"I'm not such a bad guy, and it's not like I'm raping someone." Anatoly bit his lip when he realized how the statement affected his father. "I didn't mean…"

"No, I know you didn't," Dmitry assured him, but his face was still frowned.

"She and I literally ran into each other in my room when she was cleaning it. I burst through the doors of the bathroom and knocked her down...all I had on was my towel. I couldn't help myself. I had to kiss her."

"And then you felt compelled to do what? Start having sex with her?"

"That came later," Anatoly scoffed. "She's not that easy."

"I thought you smarter than that," Dmitry said sitting back. "To get so close to someone who works for you. You saw what happened between me and Royal. You saw what it cost her. That's why she has all these crazy rules about no one being able to date as long as they work here."

"I have no intention of marrying Brigitte. We both just like each other."

"It always happens that way. Always with the intention of not doing more, but you do end up doing more, Anatoly."

"So, I can't even have a lover, now?"

"Yes, but it shouldn't be your maid or more importantly your psychotic step mother's maid," he pleaded.

"You said it. I didn't."

"What if I had been Royal? Do you realize ramifications of your actions? She would have flipped."

"Everything is not about your precious Royal," Anatoly huffed.

"I won't argue with you about that, but heed my warning, if Royal finds out, if you are not extremely careful, there will be hell to pay," Dmitry laughed. "I wish that you could have seen your face. You were as scared as schoolgirl."

"Well, I *did* think that it was Royal," Anatoly grinned.

"Then stop rushing long enough to lock door next time. You young kids screw like rabbits. Take things slow. Make her happy first, *eh*."

"I'll remember that, Casanova."

Dmitry smiled softly and sat back in his chair. His eyes narrowed in on his son. Rubbing his hands together, he sighed. "So, lay it out, Anatoly. Why should I come back, even if it is for just little while? You see that I have both of my hands full here." His smile disappeared. The lines at the sides of his eyes showed more and his age was suddenly apparent.

"Papa, this is an opportunity unlike any other," Anatoly said, changing gears.

"I've said that about each and every opportunity that has come my way."

Anatoly sighed. "This is unlike anything that we'll ever be offered again."

"How so?"

"Disgruntled Soviet Spetsnaz with 200,000 AK74 military grade weapons ready to sale in three weeks to the highest bidder along with ammunition and tactical gear."

"200,000? Impossible."

"I thought so, too. But it's the truth. They released photos and video of goods, but of course, they kept location to themselves. They are having meeting of minds tomorrow on Bardzecki's yacht right outside of Sochi."

"Why Sochi?" Dmitry immediately thought of the bridges that he had burned permanently there.

"The liaison who is facilitating the sale is coordinating this via Bardzecki, who is not a bidder but gets large fee to get us all together tomorrow. It's only open to established Russian organizations and bosses. The Spetsnaz won't sell to anyone else, which is why only mostly Vor were contacted."

"Why not Kerch? I have good contacts and good relationships in Kerch."

"Papa, they specifically said Sochi – no other cities."

Dmitry thought for a minute. "I don't like it."

"The council said that you wouldn't, that you would pass. But I know that this is good deal, and I need you to have faith in me. Once I do this deal, I have no more limitations."

"Where are you going to get the capital to pay for this?"

"I have it."

"So, why do you need me?"

"Because they said that only established Vory are allowed. I'm not credible yet in those circles."

"Nonsense. You are my son, you are boss…"

"I am not even 30 years old, papa. They don't take me seriously when it comes to moving this type of product, but they will if you come with me."

"Have you even considered that this could be a set up? If not, one word for you. Troika. 20 members led by Petrov were arrested in Majorca in one day. There are countless other ambushes. One incident was even aboard a yacht."

"Papa, I've done my research. Sorrello gave me his contacts in Eastern Europe. I talked to a man in Georgia who is working with the government there but is employed by the US."

"Sorrello is less than dependable. I was almost charged in Memphis because of his bumbling. I had to spend a fucking fortune."

"Well, he's come through lately for me. There is no bust. However, there will be surveillance."

"The predecessor of bust."

"I have plan."

Dmitry raised his brow.

Anatoly took a deep breath. "There is minimal surveillance, and we're not who they are after. Evidently, the liaison is high on some lists."

"And you want to do business with him."

"Yes. I had some people to ask around and these Spetsnaz are all trying to move the product ASAP. They've been stockpiling it for years. However, it became a little harder to do when Admiral Kurixdov retired. The last of their little operations unit retired last week after twenty years of service in the Russian Navy. This is part of their retirement plan – to sell off what they have been stealing for years. They want to move it fast and get it out of the location that it was in, because evidently without the security clearance of the last man, they can't get to it after next month."

"I've never heard of an unpatriotic Spetsnaz. It's like oxymoron. You are too young to know this, but they were instrumental to Russia during the Cold War. These are true patriots to the country. It's like suggesting there is mole in CIA. And I know there are no moles in the CIA."

"Well a few traitors exist, and they want to do business."

Dmitry shook his head in disgust. Even he had some morals. "And the liaison?"

"Bardzecki has vouched for him. He says the liaison is not a Vor, but he is most reliable."

Dmitry was impressed. This was an once-in-a-lifetime opportunity. However, what his son was asking could be treacherous to his already unstable marriage. If he went back and Royal found out, he would surely face a predicament.

Legally Royal Stone was dead. She had taken the first name of her dead sister, Chloe and was a different woman than the one he married.

If they were forced to divorce, there would be no telling how bitter things could get, especially with Anya added to the equation.

On the other hand, if he did not go and oversee something as large as this deal, his son could get killed or arrested for not knowing what to do and when. The decision would be a hard one no matter what.

He clasped his hands together and thought deeply and silently for a few minutes. Anatoly waited without moving in his chair. He had to have his father's help. There was no way possible to do this without him.

"What are you going to do about the surveillance again?" Dmitry finally asked with a furrowed brow.

"We'll be on yacht, far enough off coastline to be undetected. I know that it sounds simple, but all we have to do is change color of our hair."

Dmitry looked up. "What?"

"The Medlov's are known for our features. They identify us by our blonde hair and blue eyes. For tomorrow night only, we change the color of our hair, just for the cameras. The guy who is doing surveillance works for us."

"I'm seven feet tall. How do you plan to hide that?"

"There is no active investigation. The pictures will be stored, improperly labeled – not used. People will automatically assume that you are…"

Dmitry finished his son's statement. "Ivan."

"Exactly and they'll think its old footage. I've been assured of it."

Dmitry shook his head. "It's not that I don't trust you, but before I do this, I'm going to have my men check on this."

"I understand, but if you check it out and it's legit, will you do this for me, father?"

Dmitry shook his head. "Yes."

Chapter 5

Upset earlier by Victoria and Dmitry, Royal had taken a valium and crawled into bed before sundown, missing her appointment at the shop and refusing dinner.

Now, in the still darkness of the night, behind the cloak of her heavily covered canopy bed, she flinched through another nightmare, clawing the sheets, sweating and moaning.

Screaming aloud, she popped up shaking and curled her knees up to her chest. Tonight was a different dream. Not about just one but also the other. Without feeling for Dmitry in the large bed, she knew he was not there, but she had to find him.

Jumping out of bed, she slipped on her slippeers and bolted out of her door. She ran straight down the long carpeted hall to Anatoly's room and burst through the doors.

Anatoly immediately sat up in the bed, barechested and startled. The glimmer of his shiny Glock reflected in the moonlight.

"What's wrong?" he asked, throwing the cover from his legs. Now he wished he had listened to his father and locked the damned door, but he was waiting on Brigitte, who was still at the hospital with her sick mother.

"Where's Dmitry?" she looked around the room.

"Not here," Anatoly said curtly. "Probably in one of the guest bedrooms." He wiped his eyes. "What's wrong?" he asked again.

"I need to talk to him," she said absently.

Anatoly rolled his eyes. He stood and up and stretched. "Can we talk for a minute?"

"Not now…"

"Yes, now." Anatoly walked up to her and closed the doors behind them.

"Anatoly, did you not hear what I said? I need to talk to your father."

"I heard you," he said in a huff. "And I just said that I need to talk to you."

"Make it quick," Royal said unmoved.

"What's going on with you, huh? You're like…like crazy woman, running around here mad as hell." He circled around her.

"I don't know what you're talking about." She folded her arms.

"Oh, you don't? I don't recall you being such a bitch before you got married to my father. In fact, you weren't like this a year ago. What the fuck is going on with you?"

"I don't expect you to understand, Anatoly. And I don't owe you an explanation. What is going on with your father and me is my business."

"It's everyone's business when affects as many people as it does."

"How do our marital problems affect you? You live in Memphis, remember. You're only visiting."

"And why did he leave?"

"Because he didn't want to..."

"He. Left. For. You." He pointed at her.

"I know why he left." She flared her nostrils.

"You know. I'm going to say this and then I leave alone," he ran his hands through his hair. His broken English worsened as he became more agitated. "You used to be someone totally different, someone more for him than anyone else. Now, you're into titles, money and this proper fake-ass lifestyle instead of being the mother and wife he sacrificed for. If you ask me, he got raw end of deal with you."

"Sacrifice?" She prepared to defend.

"Don't give me your same old *Ivan-fucked-me* routine."

Royal slapped him hard in his face. Tears dropped from her eyes as she did.

His voice was lower now. He moved closer to her. "You don't think he's made sacrifices too? Whether you like it or not, he doesn't owe you anything. He just chooses to give it to you, but you know, if I really look at it, you owe him everything."

"Then it's a good thing that your view doesn't count," she said angrily. "You men are all the same. *Shake it off. Move on.* What if it were your mother, Anatoly? Or a woman you really loved? It's not that easy to get over, even when you try your best. And my best may not be up to your standards, *oh great and powerful fucking mob boss*, but it's mine. And when your father, my husband feels the need to address it, then it will be addressed with him – not his son."

Anatoly was silent.

Royal rolled her eyes but did not move. She was not the least bit intimidated by him. And after all that she had gone through, Anatoly knew it.

"*If* you love him...."

"I *do* love him."

"Then maybe you should drop the act."

"Let this be the last time that you ever feel comfortable discussing my marriage with me."

"Yes, *Mistress*," he said condescendingly as she slammed the door behind her.

Walking fast, she headed down the long corridor, opening the doors to the many bedrooms as she went. She checked Anya's room, Davyd's room, five guest rooms, and finally she came upon the last guest room at the end of the hall.

As she opened the large, embellished wood doors, it creaked. Under the moonlight, shining in from the large windows, she saw Dmitry lying in bed asleep.

Quietly, she closed the doors behind her and walked slowly over to him. He lay naked on his back with his hands planted behind the pillow. His muscles bulged from his colossal biceps, rippled down through his long, carved torso into his concrete abs that showed his vascular curves at his hips. The hair on his legs was dark and thick and covered the nearly five feet of length from his hip to his ankle. She was still amazed by his graceful temple, engulfed by his beauty.

Crawling into the bed beside him, she could not help but let her eyes linger down to his manhood snaked over the side of his thigh.

It had been so long since she had felt him inside of her, so long since she felt like a real woman. The thought made her cringe, and she paused in her anxiety for a moment as she remembered how alive she used to be.

As she turned to tap his chest and wake him, she found Dmitry staring at her. His eyes sparkled like polished diamonds in the night. Barely blinking, he pulled his hand from behind the pillow and placed his gun beside her on the nightstand.

"What's wrong, baby?" he asked, rubbing her back. "Another nightmare?"

Her voice whispered out. "Yes…" she cleared her throat. Butterflies erupted instantly. It baffled her how such a thing could happen so many years into their relationship. He still made her feel like a school girl.

"Are you afraid? Here, come and lay beside me. You're shaking."

"It wasn't about Ivan – not exactly," she said quickly. "It was more about you."

"Me? My love, I'm fine," he said finally, devouring her with a hungry, insatiable look. "But I could be better." He ran his hand down the side of her arm. Goose bumps formed. It made him smile. At least she still reacted *somewhat* to his touch.

The look in her face was sheer agony. Dmitry could see it, even in the darkness. He pulled her closer to him and pushed her long, wild hair out of her face. She looked absolutely breathtaking, even in her frantic state. Her caramel skin glowed in the darkness. Her full lips were pouty and in desperate need to be kissed. The gown had fallen over to the side of her arm, revealing the round orb of her full breasts, and suddenly Dmitry could feel the heat rising inside of him.

"I had a dream that Ivan killed you," she bit out. "He killed you, and he killed Anatoly in a lake. It was on fire." She tried to catch her breath. "He came out of the water, and he killed you both, and I had to watch. He...he was never dead, just waiting for the perfect time to strike."

Dmitry sat up in the bed a little straighter. Royal was clever. She could have found a way to overhear his conversation with Anatoly earlier, but it was highly unlikely. And the look in her face warranted that of true concern and sincerity.

He ran his hands through his golden locks and groaned. He didn't need this right now. He was hoping that she had come to make love to him, to ask him to make love to her - not to warn him of some strange portent.

"Sweetheart, Ivan is dead," he pleaded, trying to reason with her. His voice was as soft and sympathetic as always.

"I know that," Royal snapped. "But it felt real. It felt..."

"No," Dmitry snapped back. His temper reared its ugly head. "Enough of this! *Ostanovit.* He's dead, and he's not coming back!"

"I know," Royal said with tears in her eyes. "I just..."

"I have had enough," Dmitry's voice raised. "I want you to stop this. I can't take it anymore."

Royal shook her head. Tears ran down her cheeks. "If you would just listen for a damned minute!"

Dmitry got up from the bed and snatched his jogging pants. Slipping them on, he turned on the lamp and walked around to face her.

She looked at him concerned and wide-eyed, clueless to his sudden anger due to his excruciating sexual frustration.

He gritted his teeth. "I have a meeting tomorrow. My helicopter will pick me up first thing in the morning. When I get back…"

"Is it on a lake?" she interrupted.

"Listen to me, *zhenshchina*," he said sternly. "When I get back, you and I are going to go back to therapy. You aren't getting better. You're getting worse and I can't…"

"I'm not getting worse," she protested. "I came in here to tell you that you must be in some sort of danger…"

Dmitry talked over her. "You're getting worse and paranoid. I want this to stop. I'm calling the doctor and…"

"You're not listening to me!" she protested again, trying to push past him.

Dmitry blocked her. "Listen to me!" He grabbed her and shook her. "I want my wife back, damn it." He pushed her body against the bed. She fell over on the mattress.

"I haven't gone anywhere," she said crying. "Take your fucking hands off of me, Dmitry!" She tried to wheedle away. "I…I hate you!" she cried. "I came in here to tell you that you're in danger. I came in here to warn you, but you won't listen to me!" She kicked her feet.

"I have been listening to you! Every night for three years, I've been listening. And it's always about Ivan. It's like you mourn him. I can't stand it. I hate it almost as much as you hate me and Anya," he growled as he leaned in between her thighs.

Royal gasped as he held her down. She stared him in his eyes. He was only a hair away from her face. She could feel his hot chest against her body. "I don't hate my baby?" she cried. "I love Anya. She's all I've got in the world."

Dmitry was in shock. He let her go and backed away. She lay on the bed with her legs wide open, gown pulled up to her waist and visibly shaken. The sight made him instantly think of the rape. He was sure it had made her think of it as well, but her words were what destroyed him.

"After all that I have given you, you think that all you have in this world is Anya?" he asked in sheer disbelief.

She sat up in the bed. Wiping the tears from her face, she pulled her gown strap up and sniffled.

"I know that you don't love me, Dmitry. I'm just a burden that you have to bare, because I have nowhere else to go." Her bottom lip quivered. "That's why you brought Victoria here. To replace me, at least on some levels."

"Victoria? Fuck her. She's just a teacher. She's here to teach Anya. I don't give two shits about her!"

"Then why do you look at her like you do?"

"Like what?"

"Like you used to look at me," She cried. "Like before Ivan."

"I barely see her. I don't have time to look at her."

"You'll find time, won't you? You brought her here to take your mind of what I am."

"Did I?" He shook his head. "Just what the hell are you, Royal?"

Royal looked down at her shaking fingers and swallowed hard. Well, she had told Anatoly that when Dmitry brought it to her attention, she would deal with it. It was evidently time now.

"I am a drunk, addicted, crazy bitch that you accidently knocked up and was forced to marry because otherwise someone would kill me, even though you couldn't possibly want me anymore after your brother fucked me like a two-dollar whore in every God-given orifice I had, after he had broken my nose, cut me, beat me, stabbed me, sodomized me," she shook and cried. "How could anyone ever want me again? Especially his own brother, his own blood? You'd have to be insane to want me."

The breath caught in Dmitry's lungs. Sweat formed on his forehead. To hear her say those words was the purest form of torture. He exhaled finally, breathed out and deflated into a near nothingness. "Is that what you've thought? This whole time since we've come to Prague, you've thought that I saw you as damaged goods."

"I know you do. You buy me all this stuff to keep my occupied and away from you. *Royal go to shop. Royal go to city. Royal find something to do,*" she mocked him.

"I know the kind of woman you are. You are independent. You like to keep busy. I thought I was helping." His voice had lost its fury. He talked nearly in a whisper now.

"I know you detest the way that I look, but I try my best to cover it," she touched the scar on her neck. "I know that you must think about what he did every time that you touch me." She looked down. "Even now, just to be close to me is so…repulsive. And it's okay. I understand." She wiped the tears from her face. "Because I repulse my damned self. I can barely look in the mirror anymore. I can barely stand to be in my own skin. That's why I take pills. The more I sleep, the higher I am, the less I have to deal."

"Royal, no…" Dmitry said in a whisper. "But why all of sudden in the last year have things gotten so bad? Why haven't they been this bad the whole time?"

Royal tried to smile. "My little Anya really is beautiful. She's the most," she wiped tears from her cheeks. "She's the most beautiful girl that I've ever seen in my entire life, but you know, I just kept waiting for her to change –to look more like her daddy or even me. At her last birthday party, I realized that she'll always look like him. She'll always remind me, Dmitry."

"And that set you off."

"That and a hundred other things. Seeing the scars every time I take off my clothes. And you know just about six months ago my foster mother passed away. I read the newspaper there online every day. She was listed in the obituaries."

Dmitry sighed. He didn't know.

"I didn't even get a chance to say goodbye."

"I'm sure she knew that you loved her."

"And then there's me. Overall, I just feel like if I don't have my defenses up, if I'm not being a bitch at every moment, then someone will just take advantage of me again. It's hard to explain, but it's the truth." She shrugged her shoulders and spoke in a broken voice. "I'm all messed up,

Dmitry. I'm not the same girl anymore. I... I don't know who I am."

In the shadows of the dark room, Dmitry let the tears fall down his eyes. He wiped them quickly and grunted as he looked up the ceiling.

While he wouldn't tell her, he had been waiting for the moment when she would let her guard down and tell him what was wrong for a year now. In fact, he had just told Anatoly earlier that day how heartbreaking the entire situation had been for him of late. But now, he wasn't sure if he was ready for the truth.

How had he missed it? How had he not seen how badly she had been damaged? All of this time, he was focused on the way the she behaved, not looking deep enough to see how open the wound still was for her.

His massive shoulders hung in defeat. He had failed her again. This time, he had done so miserably.

"I have blamed myself for your rape for so long," he confessed. "After all, it was my brother, my blood, my sins that caused this." He took a deep breath. "I have wished so many times that things could have been different – better for you." His voice was deep, low and pained. "And worst of all, I thought that because of these things you didn't love me anymore," he smirked. "I actually thought *I* repulsed you."

Royal was shaking now, covered in tears, quivering and alone. Somehow she thought it would feel better to confess her self-contempt, but now she only felt worse. And if it were possible, she felt even more ashamed.

She avoided making eye contact, keeping her eyes on the ground. God only knew what he must think of her now that he knew she was a certifiable basket case.

"I've always loved you, Dmitry. Don't be stupid," she said coldly.

Walking over to the bed, Dmitry leaned in and scooped her up in his arms. He put her on his lap and cradled her, determined to keep the walls down that they had finally broken through tonight.

"Look at me," he said, pulling at her chin. "Hey…look at me."

She looked up nervously. He moved her long wild hair from her face and rubbed his fingers over her lips.

"How? How do I get you to see, *zhenshchina*?" Dmitry asked, kissing her forehead as he held her in his arms. "You are the best part of me." He whispered husky baritone words in her ear. "Everything that is good in my life is good because of you. There is nothing more than you. There will never be anything more than you. What Ivan did to you doesn't make you any less of a woman; it made him less than a man. And you are still the most beautiful woman that I've ever seen in my life."

"You don't have to say that, Dmitry," she said, still trembling.

"It is truth, Royal. I have never stopped wanting you. I never stopped loving or desiring every part of you whether it is your best or worst day or day in between. I don't care. You are my wife. You have been my wife since first time I make love to you, way back when you were just young girl. Now, as a woman, I love you more. I need you more than I need to breathe."

Royal looked up astonished at his words. Her mouth was open. Tears ran down her face on her neck and collarbone. "Do you really mean it, Dmitry?"

"Baby, yes, I mean it." He wiped her tears. "All this time, I thought it was me. I thought you hated my guts."

"It's never been you," Royal said, looking down. "I'm always so damned angry or so scared. I can't control how beside myself I get. Some days I just feel like I'm going to crack. I guess part of me just can't believe that he's dead. It's like he's going to just pop out of the closet or kick down the door when I least expect it. I mean I know that he's dead, but it doesn't feel like it when I dream about him every night. It's like I'm going crazy." She shook her head. "You don't know how badly I want it to go away. I don't want to feel dirty anymore," she cried.

Dmitry listened quietly, berating himself for doing such a poor job of being her husband. He had stripped her from her friends, torn her from the reach of her country, and he had all but abandoned her here in this large mansion with no one to confide in knowing she had been diagnosed with rape-related PTSD.

"I thought that you were going to leave me," Royal said softly. She looked up at him. "It's been bothering me since that woman came to my home. I don't know what I would do if you left me."

"Royal, I don't want Victoria at all." He shook his head and put his forehead on hers. "I'm not going anywhere for a long, long time."

Dmitry smiled. "All I want is you." He rubbed her cheek.

Royal shook her head, tears still flowing. "I'll try to be better," she said sincerely. "But it's going to take time. There is something wrong with me, Dmitry."

"We'll get you some help, together. When I get back, I'll go with you. I'll sit through every session. I'll hold you every night until the nightmares go away. I'll do whatever it takes. I promise."

Royal did not speak, but there was a visible burden lifting off her shoulders that showed in the brightness of her eyes. Dmitry noticed the change in her face, how the frown seemed to be not so permanent. Could it be that she had hope? He prayed that she did.

Unable to control himself, he pulled her chin towards him and kissed her soft lips. She tasted like scotch, but he didn't care. Kissing her slowly with passion enough to make her feel faint, he ran his hands through her matted hair, down her neck to her soft, silky shoulders and stopped at the orbs of her warm breasts. Then he paused to see.

For once, she didn't fight him or wince away. She pushed forward, towards his grasp. Eagerly, his fingers brushed against her nipples as he kissed her and he heard her throaty moan. The sound made him smile and erect. He felt himself growing, prodding against the satin of her gown. Without instruction, she wrapped her arms around his neck as he kissed her. Signs of improvement. He stopped and smiled at her. The long dimples in his cheek showed.

"Hey," he said breathing heavily.

"Hey," she said softly.

They looked at each other.

"I missed you," he said, clenching his jaw. The smile left. "I thought that I had lost you for good."

"I thought the same," she whispered.

He picked her up in his embrace and pulled back the thick layers of covers. Laying her down on the bed, he looked at her body and shook his head.

"I was just getting on to Anatoly earlier about taking it slow. For once, I know how he feels."

"Taking it slow with whom?"

"Nobody." He stood beside the bed. "Hold on a minute. Let me…lock the door." He brushed his hands through his curly locks again and walked over to the door. After he locked it, he returned to her and crawled into the bed beside her.

She watched him as he did. Her eyes were inquisitive. For once, she almost wanted him to take her. There was some strange spark of arousal that she had not felt in nearly a year.

Normally, he would have struck. He would have used the opportunity to make her fulfill all of his desires, but he knew how fragile she was. What he needed was his wife naked and open to all of his carnal needs that only seemed to multiply every time that he looked at her body in that satin gown. However, what she needed was someone to show her that everything would be alright and not just for a night but for the rest of her life.

He had to take it slow to prove to her that he could help bring her out of her deep depression. Also, he was certain that he didn't have the patience to be gentle at the very moment. It would be wisest to wait until he returned home from his trip to make love to her. Tonight, he might scare her, might hurt her or remind her like before of the one man in the world he wished hadn't existed.

Pulling her into his chest and his steely erection, he wrapped his long, muscular arms around her and listened to her heartbeat. She crawled into chest and yawned. Like a sleepy cat, she purred and dug in for a long nap.

"You don't want to make love to me?" she asked, looking across the room at the chaise lounge.

"Yes," he whispered.

"Then why don't you?"

"It's not always about me, *eh*?"

"You've got that right," she said smiling. "But it's not always about me either.

Dmitry lifted his brow. A selfless word from Royal? She was coming around. He pulled her closer into his chest and put his hot lips to her ear. The contact felt like electricity on her skin.

"I will make it all about you when I get back from my meeting," he said recognizing the chemistry between them. He raised his large arm and planted in front of her and sat up a little. "I can't even tell you what I want to do, but if you let me show you…"

Royal turned around and faced him. Her brown eyes sparkled as they looked up at him under dark thick lashes. "Why can't you tell me?"

Dmitry looked down, somewhat ashamed. "I don't want to scare you."

"It's not you who scares me, Dmitry. It's the reminder of him." She rolled her eyes. "I've never been afraid of you?"

"No?" Dmitry asked, raising a brow.

"No."

"Really, well what's this then?" he asked, showing her an old knife wound in his arm from where she had stabbed him when she first found out about his ties to the mafiya.

"I overreacted," she said smiling. She couldn't help but laugh. Neither could he.

"I haven't been afraid of you since, should I say," she corrected.

"Well that makes one of us. I've been scared shitless of you since then."

She smiled again, revealing white pearly teeth as she did.

Dmitry sighed. "God, you're beautiful."

Royal shook her head. "Not as beautiful as you."

Chapter 6

When his jet touched down in Sochi, Russia, Dmitry was engulfed in deep thought about his wife and her confessions to him the night before.

He sat alone in the back with his legs crossed and his chin buried in his hand as he looked out of the window. Even many hours later, he could smell her cologne on him. He had even avoided taking a shower just to keep her scent on him as long as possible.

Royal's confession had awakened the passion in him yet again. Letting her guard down had been the best thing she could have done for the both of them. In fact, the entire experience was magical and oddly enough with no sex involved.

However, she had kissed him for hours – like they had never kissed before. She allowed him to touch her in places that before would have sent her into a frenzy. Her eyes were bright in the moonlight, almost as bright as her angelic smile. His heart fluttered. Royal was back.

"Now you really look like the bastard, papa," Anatoly said, making his way to the back of the jet.

Dmitry looked up and snapped out of his daze. "Don't remind me. Let's just get this over with so that I can get this shit out of my hair and off my eyebrows. I feel like idiot." He slipped on his Aviator shades.

"The car is waiting outside for us."

Anatoly turned around and headed off the plane behind the bodyguards. "Since this is not as official, I was hoping that we could ride in the same car for once."

Dmitry stood up and made his way off the plane. As he did so, his staff and men looked on amazed at his transformation. He went from a blonde giant to dark, sinister brunette with piercing looks that mirrored his dead brother, Ivan.

Getting in the back of the Bentley, he checked his phone and looked over at his son. He had to continue to remind himself of why he was doing this. It was only after they had left the salon, after his transformation, that he realized how traumatized his wife must be.

When he looked in the mirror after his hair color had been changed, he nearly tore out his own eyes. He was Ivan Medlov incarnate, and while the look would surely benefit his son's new project, it was killing him inside.

"Are you sure about this, Anatoly?"

"I thought that we had discussed this. Of course, I'm sure. Trust me, papa."

"Alright," Dmitry said, trying to relax.

"Are you...uh...listening to this?" Anatoly asked, reaching into his Louis Vuitton backpack.

"No," Dmitry said in a daze again. "Listen to whatever you like."

Anatoly passed the bodyguard a CD. "Play this," he said.

The man took it quickly and turned off the local Russian radio station. Suddenly, Lil Wayne came on the radio. Anatoly gave a bright smile as he heard the beat drop and guitars screaming. The tempo filled the car with heart-pounding music.

Dmitry stopped looking out of the window and looked over at Anatoly with a furrowed brow.

"Hey, I'm boss now, remember?," Anatoly smiled.

"What kind of shit is this?"

"Wheezy." Anatoly's accent became thicker.

"It's....it's rap music," Dmitry said, holding his head. "It's like nails against chalk board. Please, please. Turn off."

"What's wrong with rap music?" Anatoly laughed. His father was visibly in pain. The music stopped.

"What isn't?" Dmitry ran his fingers over the side consul and let down the window to breathe. Wheezy had almost given him a heart attack. "Save for when I'm not in car, *eh*."

***

Brigitte knocked on Mistress Medlov's door several time before she entered. Oddly enough there was no answer. She came through the double doors with her back to the bed as she pulled in the tray of breakfast food.

However, when she turned around, she realized that she was alone in the room. She looked around curiously. In the last year, she had not come into the room one morning that the Mistress was not in bed, knotted in sheets with a glass of scotch on her nightstand.

"Mistress Medlov?" Brigitte called.

She looked in the large bathroom, in Dmitry's closet, in both of Royal's closets and in the sitting room connected to the bedroom and found no one there. It was not her place to fetch her, but she felt the sudden urge to turn and run out of the room calling after Davyd.

***

Royal was still wrapped in the covers that smelled like her husband in the guest room where Dmitry had left her. She slept heavily, uninterrupted by nightmares and with a slight grin on her face.

Davyd looked in on her just to make sure that she was okay. After Brigitte had come into the great room sweaty and wide-eyed, he had no choice. Evidently, the poor girl had run all the way from the Mistress's bedroom on the second floor to the great room on the first floor. Thousands upon thousands of concrete and marble feet were in between the two locations.

Davyd was nearly as worried if not more worried when Brigitte explained Royal's absence from her room. Running to the security office, he rewound video from the night before and saw her go into bedroom with her husband after she left Anatoly's room. A feeling of relief for several reasons overcame him. Still he felt the need to check in on her.

Royal slept until noon. When she finally woke up from her peaceful slumber, for the first time in over a year, she was not sweaty, was not hung over and was not angry.

Mouth dry, she pulled the covers from her body and made her way to the bathroom. She couldn't help but smile at her reflection in the mirror. It was not because she thought she was anymore beautiful, but because she could still smell her husband on her skin. She could still hear the soft beautiful words he had whispered in her ear the night before. She held herself tight and took a deep breath. She had promised to do better and be better. And she would keep her promise.

***

Victoria had the day off and planned to spend her Saturday out in the city of Prague finding a way to let her hair down.

Being prim and proper every single day with no release had gotten really old and being holed up in the Medlov's chateau only made her more anxious for some excitement. She almost understood why the mistress was such a pain.

At first, she had planned on spending the day in the courtyard only a few feet from Dmitry's study playing with Anya and in his view, waiting for the moment when his daughter would draw him out to talk to them. But when she found out that he had hopped a helicopter out of happy town, she had no need to spend unneeded hours playing with his overly-smart three-year old..

The city of Prague was alive today. After lunch at Dmitry's posh Russian restaurant, she headed down on the cobblestone streets of Prague 1 to visit Royal Flush.

As soon as Victoria entered the swank boutique, she heard John Mayer's *Heartbreak Warfare* and smelled expensive perfumes floating through the air. The entire shop was painted in a warm royal blue with silver and gold mirrors and pictures of different cities and designers on the wall.

A huge crystal chandelier hung from the center of the ceiling above a large circular blue velvet chaise lounge and illuminated the room with reflections of crystal and gold.

Two slender women, who could have easily passed for models, stood behind the counter in matching black dresses with bright smiles. The redhead walked up to Victoria.

"Welcome to Royal Flush," she said in an English accent. "My name is Lola. May I help you find something, or are you just looking today?"

"Just looking," Victoria said, impressed with the shop. It was a mix of old world opulence and new world technology. "I'm actually Mrs. Medlov's daughter's teacher, Victoria. I figured on my day off, I would just stop by and check out the boutique."

The redhead raised her brow as if this wasn't the first time that she heard the name. "Oh, you're Anya's teacher." There was visible smirk on her face. "Well, please let us know if we can get anything for you. Would you like some water or maybe a glass of champagne while you shop?"

"Sure. I'll take a glass of bubbly," she said curiously.

The redhead looked over at the blonde woman and raised her finger. "One please," she said before she moved out of Victoria's way. "Please make comfortable."

I bet ten dollars that bitch has been talking bad about me, Victoria thought to herself as she took the glass from the woman. She looked around at the racks of name brand clothes and nearly choked. $5,000 for a dress, $7,000 for a suit. Who were they kidding?

Gulping down the champagne, she looked around for the clearance rack. Oddly enough, there was not one. Snooty ass, she thought shaking her head. Within in minutes, she decided that Royal Flush was not the place for her or her budget.

Setting the glass on the counter before she left, she waved at the women and headed out the door as a group of well-dressed women in furs came through the door speaking to each other in French. As she looked back, she saw the two sales women together laughing and talking under her breath.

"Thank you for shopping at Royal Flush," the woman said, when she realized that Victoria was leaving.

"Before I leave," Victoria said, turning around. "Where can I go have a drink in a sort of party-like atmosphere during the day? This is Prague, right? You guys know how to have a little fun here, don't you?"

Lola pulled herself away from her associate and walked over to Victoria. She put her hands on her hip. "Party-like?"

"Party-like," Victoria said, wiping her nose. "From the look of you, I can tell that you know. You can't naturally be a size two can you?"

The woman smiled at the ill-formed compliment. "There is a pub not far from here off of LeBeauch Lane. It's called the Rector. You can order a drink and whatever else you need, but it's expensive. Because of the area, you're going to pay way more than market value."

"Well, I don't mind paying for that," Victoria said smirking.

"Ask for Myneau," she said in a little warmer tone to Victoria "He'll help you out."

With that Victoria headed out. She hadn't had a serious release since she got there. Customs was too much of risk to get good shit through. It would be nice to do a few lines and get some pills for later.

***

A breathtaking Sunset was on the horizon of the Russian Riviera by the time that Dmitry settled into his exclusive suite at the Rodina Hotel.

With the curtains pulled to see the Black Sea and the parade of fine yachts as they sailed by, he poured himself a nice strong glass of vodka and opened his laptop. The meeting would not be for another two hours. It would give him just enough time to take a bath and call Royal.

Even after a hectic day, he still could not take his mind off of her. How he longed to be with her now. He wanted to hear her voice, feel her hot body against his again, smell her perfume and feel her long hair rub over him. The thought of her oddly enough gave him an uncompromising hard on. He looked down at his rising pants and sighed.

"Royal, you're killing me," he said aloud, taking a sip from the crystal goblet.

The sun slipped into his room as it reflected on the water. Crisp air waved the soft curtains and shined on his bright eyes. They flickered in the mirror across the room as he looked at himself.

He was getting old. He could see the gray in hair when the stylist had pulled through his gold locks earlier. And he could see the lines even more pronounced now on the sides of his eyes.

Time was no longer on his side. That was why he had to do this for his son, even though he was going against his sacred vows to his young wife.

Anatoly had a chance to make a true name for himself – something that would be more respected by his peers than a legacy.

Closing his eyes, he rested his head back on the chocolate leather chair and tried to relax.

***

While Dmitry was resting, Anatoly was downstairs with his bodyguards having drinks at the Black Magnolia. With only a few people in the restaurant, he had a clear view of a huddle of young blondes eyeing him from across the room. They looked like trouble, like fun. He ordered them drinks and had them sent over.

"I think she wants you, boss," his bodyguard, Vasily, said smiling.

"Which one?" Anatoly asked looking at the girls as they waved thanks over to him. "I don't see how my father does it. He's faithful to one woman," he shook his head. "One woman." He put up his index finger.

"What's wrong with that," Vasily asked.

"Well you can't have all of them if you're busy pleasing *one*," Anatoly said, grinning as the women got up from their seats and headed towards them.

Anatoly had never committed to Brigitte, nor did he plan to anytime soon. He was Vor – and not just any Vor. He was boss. His father had thrown away the freedom that came with such a prestigious honor.

Not being allowed to marry or have children simply meant that he never had to worry about being tied down. There was no one to argue with or lie to about his whereabouts, no one to spend late nights lamenting over and no one to answer to except God and council.

He smiled at the thought. These women were like so many. They saw the expensive clothes, the entourage of men, the watches, the cars and the attention. They all wanted to be a part of it. He was happy to oblige them…for the night.

s the sun set in Prague, Victoria pulled up to the private drive of the Chateau as high as a kite from doing coke lines in the back room of the restaurant with some shady characters she had met through Ryno. Maybe now, she could finally stomach the Medlov clan for another week before she headed back to her new haven.

Lanterns hung beside the closed iron gate and two cameras focused in on the car. After a moment, the gates opened, and she dashed down the road with the top down in one of the family's cars, a sleek silver Maserati GranCabrio.

Unbelievably, the Mistress had allowed her to borrow it. She knew that Mistress Medlov didn't want to, but the prospect of getting her out of the house was too exciting for the uptight witch to resist. When Victoria had asked her about borrowing a vehicle, the mistress had thrown her the keys and said simply, "it's the last car on the left wing of the garage." With that she sashayed out of the room with her daughter and disappeared down the hall.

After parking the car, Victoria grabbed a few bags out of the trunk and headed inside the house. To her surprise, Anya was nowhere to be found. Evidently, Mistress Medlov had spent the entire day with her daughter instead of curled up in her bed like a hermit. There were even fresh flowers throughout all of the foyers. She walked in the darkness down the marble hallway to the stairs leading to her room. As she made it to the steps, she heard a voice behind her.

"Victoria," Royal said softly.

"Yes ma'am," Victoria answered, turning around slowly. She could see the tall woman standing down the hall. Even in the darkness, she looked stately in a slender skirt and turtleneck.

"I'd like to talk to you, if you're not too busy…now," Royal hit the light fixture and lit up the dark corridor. "Would you mind meeting me in my study?"

"Of course," she backed away from the stairs and followed Mistress Medlov with the bags and her purse still in her hand.

Victoria had no idea that the mistress had a study, too. Where was it? She thought that she had committed every room on the first floor to memory.

Victoria followed her with at least ten feet between them past Dmitry's study, past the great room and gym to a pair of white double doors at the very end of the hall in the corner.

Royal unlocked the doors and opened them for Victoria. "After you," she said waiting. Closing the doors behind them, she offered Victoria a seat and sat down behind the massive white oak credenza.

"Would you like some tea?" Royal offered graciously. She poured herself a large glass and set it beside her.

"No," Victoria said, looking for the booze. It surprised her that the mistress wasn't drunk tonight, especially with Dmitry away from home. "Do you have something stronger?"

Royal raised her brow and smiled. "I'm sure I do, but for now, let's talk about why I wanted to speak with you." She sighed. "Victoria, I want to write you a letter of recommendation."

"Really," Victoria was speechless.

"Yes, for your next assignment. You see, when you came here, we had unresolved issues that you had nothing to do with. Since you have come here, we have resolved those issues and in the process have realized that we are no longer in need of your services."

Victoria was silent.

"So, we are going to pay you in full for your entire contract, provide you with a letter of recommendation and send you on your way…tomorrow."

"I see."

Royal waited for a response.

"If I may ask, when was this decision made?"

Royal did not see the relevance but chose to answer. "I made the decision today, and I will discuss it with Dmitry tonight when he returns, but trust me the decision is final."

"I understand." Victoria smiled. "Well thank you for the opportunity, Mrs. Medlov. It has been my pleasure. Since I'll be leaving tomorrow, do you mind if we spend a while talking about my progress with Anya?"

Royal was relieved that there was no opposition. "Sure. Now that we've gotten that out of the way, what type of stronger drink would you like?"

"Umm....scotch sounds nice. Do you have any?"

"Of course. I'll be right back."

Royal left the room quietly and walked down the hall to the great room to grab a bottle of scotch. Victoria listened carefully for the click of her stilettos then reached into her purse and pulled out a vile of cocaine. Dropping a little more than a gram into Royal's tea, she swished around the contents to make sure it could not be detected and slipped the vile back in her purse. Soon after, Royal returned with a crystal vase of scotch and poured Victoria a glass.

"Sorry it took so long. Davyd must have put it away."

Royal sat back down and sighed. This hadn't been so bad. Originally, she thought that because of the short notice, there might be a conflict, but alas it had not. She smiled at Victoria, and then noticed her eyes were dilated.

"Are you alright, Victoria?" Royal asked curiously. "You look…high."

Victoria laughed. "No. I had a few drinks earlier, a lot earlier, but I'm fine."

"You didn't drink and drive, did you?"

"Honestly, Mrs. Medlov, I only had two drinks earlier, and I waited a couple of hours to drive. I just haven't had anything to drink since I've been here considering my position. Now that I'm leaving, I figured I might as well have another."

"I guess you're right," Royal relaxed. "What's a few drinks, huh?"

***

The dark waters on the Black Sea were heavy with waves passing by in silent melodic symphony as the large yacht navigated on the coastline under the cover of night. Dmitry stood on the deck looking over at the water as the other men talked cheerfully among themselves.

In his own torture, he continued to think of Royal. Some strange force was pulling him back home to her, so much in fact, it was impossible for him to concentrate. It had been agony to get dressed and come out here with men he had vowed to the only person who had truly loved him to never see again.

His mind was twisted around a collage of thoughts of Royal, of what she had been through, of what they had both sacrificed to walk away from this life, and yet here he was again being what he denied he was for almost three years…a Vor.

For the others at the meeting, it was a pleasure to have the great Dmitry Medlov back in their midst, and a pleasure to know that the name would be carried on by his trusted son, Anatoly. The group had received them both happily and was not surprised to know that largest international gunrunners in the business were interested in this *once-in-a-lifetime* opportunity. Once they were escorted with their entourage of men on to the yacht, there was no question in most of their minds that if the Medlov's wanted this business, they would get it.

Anatoly was the center of attention. The men swarmed around him, quizzing him on his knowledge of global interaction among the Vory and his position on new business like cybercrime and old business like human trafficking.

For Anatoly, this was a coming out party of sorts. While he had been the big fish in the little pond of the United States, there was evidently a lot more business outside of the secure borders of the free world.

As the crowd dissipated, Anatoly found his way over to his father. He was tower of silence tonight only nodding and smiling at the men in his normal gentle fashion but much more introverted than usual.

Dmitry stood with a glass of vodka in a black suit that only made him look taller and more regal. His dark hair gleamed with luster and his eyes pierced through all that he bothered to notice.

"Papa, what is the matter?" Anatoly asked, sitting in the chair by where his father stood.

"Nothing. I am here to support you. You are the guest of honor tonight. There is no need for me to make show."

"They all are excited to see you. I've heard a hundred stories since I got here about all that you've done as boss. I have so much to live up to," Anatoly seemed proud.

"Well, the more they like you, the better, son. I have spoken with my contacts. The transaction is legit. However, all you do tonight is make bid. There is nothing more until the seller contacts the bidder he is most interested in doing business with after checking all of his references."

"So after this, we wait?"

"In just awhile, they'll ask you for your bid. You type it into computer, confirm it with liaison, and then you enjoy the rest of night. We are not foot soldiers. We have done what we have come to do. After they have made their decision, they will contact you. So, don't be surprised if you hear from them in the morning, or you never hear from them again."

Anatoly sighed. "So cut and dry."

"We are not men who like our time to be wasted. This process has been perfected over time to ensure confidentially and efficiency."

"So what's with you? Besides this, what is going on in that very complicated brain of yours?"

Dmitry sighed. "I want to go home. After you make bid, I've arranged for my jet to be fueled, and I fly out of here. You should stay and get to know the men."

"Did something happen?"

"Yes," Dmitry smiled and turned toward his son. "She's coming around."

"It took long enough." He sat back in his seat more relaxed. Of course, it had to be about Royal. It was all the man ever thought of anymore. Royal. Anya. Royal.

"It took time that it needed," Dmitry said, shaking his head. "You are so young. Women don't come around when you want them to; they come around when it's time."

"For me, women cum when I've worked hard enough," Anatoly grinned.

"Are you being safe, Casa Nova?" Dmitry's blue eyes narrowed.

"Yes. Of course. I don't want to get package," Anatoly grinned, mirroring the same hauntingly beautiful looks.

Dmitry shook his head. His dimples showed. "I remember time when I was just like you. Be careful, *eh*. There is only so much Anatoly to go around."

The crowd silenced suddenly, and a tall blonde woman in a tailored black suit walked out with a computer. She placed it carefully on the table and typed in a password.

"Gentlemen, we are ready to begin bids," she said in a Russian accent.

"Like clockwork," Dmitry whispered.

***

Royal checked on Anya once last time before she headed to her room. In a flash of heat, she felt her vision began to blur. For the life of her, she didn't understand why. She had after all not had a drink or taken any valium today. She had promised Dmitry. And she wanted to do better for the prospect of a better life with the family that she owed everything. Still, she felt confused, high and jittery.

Going into her bedroom, she closed the door and watched her hand slide down the door. There were four hands instead of one.

Lying down on the bed, she looked up at the ceiling and closed her eyes. She had gotten high once in junior high. The strange feeling she was experiences now, felt mildly like it, only stronger.

Biting her lip, she ran her fingers down her blouse and pulled it up off her skin. She had to get out of these clothes, had to get out of her skin.

She ran her fingers down her burning body and sighed as the hard nails dug into her flesh. *Ahh.* That felt…good.

She sat up quickly. Something was wrong. Maybe she was having withdrawal from being clean for a day – valium, no alcohol. No. She shook her head at the thought. This was something else. The lights seemed to shine directly into her eyes, blinding her.

Getting off the bed, she went and turned off the light. In the darkness, she stood half-dressed and afraid. Something was happening to her.

Her heart raced. Her skin crawled. The room spun so fast until she had to close her eyes to make it stop. Placing her hands on her ears, she took deep breaths. *Calm down!* she commanded herself. But the confusion had taken on a life of its own.

Desperate she ran into closet, hitting her shoulder on the door and falling down on the flor. She looked up at the light disoriented. Pulling herself up off the ground, she went to her drawer and pulled out a hidden bottle of vodka.

She just needed something to calm down. Opening the bottle, she turned it up and drank it quickly. Wiping her mouth, she laid back down on the ground and took a deep breath. *That wasn't smart,* she thought to herself as the room began to spin.

Tears ran down her face. Why she didn't know, but suddenly, she could see Ivan. She could feel him on her skin.

"No," she said breathing hard.

"No...no....no!" She pulled her skirt, ripping it as she did so. Was she hallucinating? She could smell his cologne, hear his deep, baritone voice, feel him. "No!" she screamed. "IVAN!"

Her anxiety escalated within seconds and she found herself nearly hyperventilating in the closet, where no one could hear her or save her from herself. Holding herself tight, she rocked in the closet, nearly naked and screaming.

Chapter 8

Dmitry couldn't wait. The urgency in his chest would no longer let him. He urged the men to dock, and he left nearly in a run back to the hotel. He had tried to call Royal several times on her personal cell, yet no one answered. She always answered. He ran up to his room, grabbed his laptop and left his clothes. A car was waiting for him at the steps of the hotel. He jumped in and had the chauffeur hightail it to the airport. Within thirty minutes, he was on his jet.

The flight had been less than torturous. When he arrived in Prague, he was severely distressed, though he didn't know why. He couldn't move fast enough. He had left all of his clothes back in Sochi along with his Rolex and his shoes in a fit of a rush.

When the jet landed, he was on the helicopter in minutes and only a short distance away from his wife. He dialed Davyd but did not get an answer. Evidently he was asleep. He finally called the house phone. Surprisingly, Victoria answered.

"Victoria!" Dmitry sat up.

"Yes," Victoria said softly.

"Is…is Royal…I mean, is my wife alright?"

"Yeah. She went to bed nearly an hour ago. I was just downstairs, and I heard the phone ring. I hope you don't mind me answering it."

"No, of course not. Where is Davyd?"

"I think he's asleep. He checked everything right after Royal went up to her room."

"Well, I am not far from home. Can you let her know that I'm on my way, and I look a little different? I don't want to scare her."

"Scare her?"

"Da Da. Tell her I don't quite look myself. She won't answer her phone, but she needs to know before I get there. I don't want to startle her."

"Oh…okay." Victoria rolled her eyes. He treated Mrs. Medlov like she was such big shit. Who cared what he looked like? "If you don't mind, I'll run upstairs to the second floor and tell her now," she said.

"That would be wonderful," Dmitry sat back more relaxed. "I'll be home very soon."

"Good," Victoria said. *Counting on it*, she thought to herself as she hung up the phone.

Instead of going to tell Royal, she sprayed her perfume on and made sure that her hair was perfect. She had waited for Davyd to go to bed, waited for the help to retire, waited for Dmitry to come home. If she was going to have a chance with him, it would have to be tonight. Mrs. Medlov, after all, had plans of getting rid of her first thing in the morning.

Minutes later, the helicopter landed in the courtyard, blowing debris around in twisters of wind as hit the ground with lights shining right into the chateau. Dmitry stepped out of the helicopter with his laptop and saw Royal's window open. She was standing in it, nearly naked. He looked up at her curiously and then ran to the front door.

Royal closed the curtain as the helicopter took off. She knew it. Ivan wasn't dead. Tears ran down her eyes. Shaking, she ran out of her room as fast as she could, still half-dressed, down the hall to her daughter's room. She burst through the door and picked her sleeping daughter up.

"Mommy?" Anya asked afraid as she clutched her mother's neck.

"We have to go, baby," Royal whispered, still shaking. "Mommy has to get you to safety."

Running with her daughter in her arms, she sprinted to Anatoly's room and pulled open the dresser drawers. Throwing clothes, she finally pulled out a large gun and cocked it.

"Stay here," Royal ordered, opening up Anatoly's closet. "Hide, baby, until I come back for you." Tears ran down her face. She bent down to her crying child and kissed her red cheeks. "I love you." Pushing her daughter into the closet, she locked it behind her and headed back out of the room with the gun in her hand.

Dmitry was confused and alarmed by the look of his wife. Victoria opened the large doors to greet him, but he whisked past her and ran up the long stairway. His feet could barely keep up with his speed.

"Royal!" he shouted as he arrived on the second floor.

He looked down the long, dark corridor and saw her coming towards him. Her silhouette was beautiful. Long, dark hair wrapped around her nearly naked body. In a pair of stilettos and a black silk slip, she raised what appeared to be a gun as she ran towards him.

He squinted and then hit the light switch to see the gun raised.

"Royal!" he shouted as he ducked.

Bullets whizzed past him. He took cover in the doorway.

"Ivan, you son of bitch! I knew it! Where is my husband?" she screamed, walking fast towards him. "If you killed him!"

"Baby, it's me!" Dmitry said as he saw Davyd come running up the stairs with guns in both hands. He signaled him not to shoot.

"Dmitry?" he said, making his way to his boss. He barely missed being shot as he did.

"Royal has gone mad," Dmitry said, reaching into his holster and pulling out his gun.

"Are you going to shoot her?" Davyd asked mortified.

"No! I want to make sure that she knows I'm not armed."

"Come out, you coward!" she ordered, shooting and blowing out a chunk of the wall. "You came here for me and my baby? I'm going to kill you myself! This time I'll know for sure that you're dead!" She shot again.

"Fuck," Dmitry said ducking. "Royal it's me. I...I changed my hair color. I wanted to try something new for you. It was way to make you stop always thinking of Ivan and maybe think of Anya more as mine." It was amazing what kind of lies he could come up with at gun point.

He and Davyd both heard the shots getting closer.

"Maybe she'll run out of bullets," Davyd hoped.

They heard her duck behind a door and reload. The magazine hit the floor as she shoved another inside the gun.

"Not a chance," Dmitry said. He closed his eyes and took a deep breath. Finally, he handed Davyd the gun and shook his head. "Don't shoot her, no matter what," he said solemnly.

"You can't go out there," Davyd said, holding him back.

"I have to," Dmitry growled, pulling away his hand. "I have to. It's my fault."

Royal reloaded and walked closer, making her way down the long corridor. "Come out!" she screamed, shooting another round with tears in her eyes.

Dmitry moved from behind the door and stood in the hallway. "Royal, it's me. It's Dmitry. Ivan is dead, sweetheart. Just like we discussed last night."

Royal had the gun pointed at him. Even with many feet between them, she could hear something different in his voice, something familiar. She shook her head and grasped the gun with both hands.

"Liar!" she screamed.

"I came home like I promised." Dmitry raised his hands. "Look, no guns, baby." He took off his coat.

"Royal, it's Dmitry!" Davyd shouted. "It's Dmitry! God, can't you see that! You're about to kill your own husband!"

The room was still spinning. Royal wiped the tears and held the gun sturdy. *Could it be?* She walked closer towards him.

"Don't you fucking move!" she commanded.

"I won't," Dmitry said with his hands in the air.

In a mean sway, Royal advanced towards him. Tears in her eyes, sweating and shaking, she got closer. As she did so, her eyes fluttered. It was Dmitry! The gun began to shake. She looked up at her husband in the eyes.

By now, the floor was surrounded with men with guns, all unsure if they should point it at the mistress of the house or watch their boss die.

Dmitry stood still. Davyd stood only steps behind him, pleading with her and behind him Stepan stood with several other men.

When Royal was only a few feet from Dmitry, she took a deep breath. It was him. She clicked the safety on and dropped the gun in disbelief. Putting her hands over her mouth, she started to cry.

"Oh my God. I'm so sorry," she said in disgust. "I'm so sorry. I didn't know." Tears fell down her cheeks on to her collar bone.

Dmitry put his hands down and sighed. His heart was nearly in his throat. He had never imagined dying at his wife's hands before. He could handle it from anyone except her.

He walked closer to her and saw that she was completely distraught, but something else was wrong. Her pupils were dilated. Her skin was clammy and shaking.

"Baby," he said sympathetically.

As he reached for her, she fainted.

Catching her before she hit the ground, he picked her up and waved off his men. "She's alright," he said, checking her pulse. "Davyd!" he looked behind him. "Call the doctor. Tell him to get over here right now."

The house seemed to move in slow motion as Davyd ran passed Dmitry to find Anya. He and Stepan ran to her room and found it empty. Instinctively, Davyd ran to Anatoly's room, where he heard the young child screaming and beating on the closet door to get out. He didn't have a key, so he told her stand back and kicked it open.

Terrified, the girl stood in the back of the closet, screaming out for her mommy. He picked her up and held her tight as he whispered sweet, calming words into her ear.

Dmitry took his wife into their bedroom and closed the door. Carefully, he laid her on the bed and covered her in the sheets. He smelled vodka all over her. He couldn't understand. She had promised, and Royal would never break her promise.

He sat beside her on the bed with his hands covering his face. He had failed her again. As he looked up, he caught a glimpse of himself in the mirror across he room. All that he could see was Ivan.

Disgusted, he got up from the bed and wiped the tears from his eyes.

Davyd walked in and stopped at the doorway. He looked over at the bed to Royal.

"Anya is back in her room. I had Victoria stay in there with her until she falls back to sleep," he informed his boss.

"I'll be in to check on her in a minute," Dmitry said drained. "Is she physically hurt, Davyd?"

"No. She's just shook up. Is Royal going to be alright?" Davyd asked.

Dmitry looked over at Royal. "I don't know."

"Well to help things, you might want to do something with that hair, *eh*?"

Dmitry sighed and smirked. "I think it's what set her off. She told me before I left that she felt like he would just show up one day."

"Looks like her worst fears came true. See to your wife. I'll take care of everything else," Davyd said, closing the door behind him."

Dmitry went into the bathroom and closed the door behind him. He looked in the mirror in sheer disgust. If he had just stayed, none of this would have happened. Royal had finally started to open up and what did he do? He brought it all back to her doorstep.

Reaching into the cupboard, he pulled out a black container and opened it to find a pair of unused clippers.

He plugged them in, leaned over into the sink and pulled the hair back off of his forehead. Running his thumb over the switch, he ran them down the middle of his wavy hair and watched it fall into the water basin.

Chapter 9

Victoria waited with Anya until she fell asleep. She sat quietly in the chair in the corner of the bedroom in the dark wondering how in the hell things had gotten so out of the control. She was supposed to be mounting Dmitry at this very moment in the silence of a quiet mansion.

Now, there were maids and a butler pulling bullets out of the wall. The letter of recommendation was definitely out of the question along with the possibility of a full year's pay. All she could hope was that Dmitry wouldn't ask her if she had told Mrs. Medlov about his change or not. She didn't see why changing his hair color was such a big deal, and she wondered why he had continued to call her Royal. She thought the woman's name was Chloe.

The bedroom door opened slowly, and she saw a massive frame darkening the entryway. It was Dmitry. He came in without acknowledging her presence and went over to his daughter. Bending down on his knees, he ran his hands through her hair. Anya sniffled at little and then turned her back to him and continued to sleep.

Dmitry crumpled over from exhaustion and sighed. As he did so, he caught a glimpse of Victoria. He looked over at her quickly.

"Victoria?"

"Yes, sir?"

"I need to talk to you," he said, standing up. "Meet me in my study. I'll be down in a minute."

"Yes, sir," she repeated.

She noticed his drastic change from a curly brunette to now a short, nearly bald fade. She was still confused as to why his changing his hair color had created a near massacre of the entire household. *Yet another mystery of this already elusive family.*

Victoria left the room quickly and walked through the long hall, past the staff that hurriedly cleaned the mess as Stepan oversaw them.

In need of another hit, she ducked into the guest bathroom and closed the door. Taking out the vile in her bra, she emptied the last of the cocaine on her hand and snorted it up.

Sucking in hard through her nostrils, she wiped her nose quickly and looked in the mirror.

It was time to shine. If she was ever going to make a move, it would have to be now. She would be understanding and gentle with Dmitry, give him a shoulder to cry on and give her regrets for having to leave, as she was sure that he did not know already of his wife's decision to end her contract. She would watch him grow infuriated that Royal had usurped him, and then she would throw herself at his mercy.

By the time Mistress Medlov woke up from her slumber, Victoria would have Dmitry right where she wanted him – in between her thighs. She smiled at the thought and licked her lips.

Pushing her bra up and positioning her breasts where they showed more, she sprayed a little more perfume, fixed her hair and then left the bathroom, headed for Dmitry's study. When she arrived, he was already there sitting by the fireplace. She came in and closed the door quietly. He looked up at her as she did so.

"Please have a seat," he said in a deep baritone.

His voice sent chills through her aroused body.

"Alright," she said, taking the seat closest to him.

Rubbing his temples, he sat back in the chair with his eyes planted on her. He hated dealing with women. In truth, he despised a sneaky woman more than any other being in the world. It was too much of a reminder of his mother and his late sister-in-law.

"Did you tell my wife what I asked?" He watched her cross her legs.

"No," Victoria said, swallowing hard. "I couldn't find her, sir. I went looking every-where."

"Everywhere?"

"Yes, sir?"

"My house is rather large. How could you look *everywhere* and still be at the front door to open it when I arrived home?"

"The bottom floor was the last place that I looked."

"I see." His jaw clenched tighter.

"I had no idea that something so small would create such a horrible …catastrophe."

"Of course not. How could you?"

He sat up in his seat and leaned towards her. "Your eyes…they're dilated like my wife's." He smiled and tilted his head. "Did you two get into something tonight?"

"No, sir. We had one drink earlier. She fixed them for us right after she told me that tomorrow would be my last day here."

Dmitry didn't blink. "Why did she tell you that?"

"She said that you all had reached a decision together and my contract would be paid in-full, and I would be expected to leave."

Dmitry raised his brow. "Well, she's correct. Your contract has ended, and you will be paid in full…*after* I get to the bottom of this."

Victoria's heart raced. "Bottom of what, sir? You can't believe that I had anything to do with what just happened upstairs?"

"But…I do believe that you had something to do with what happened upstairs whether knowingly or unknowingly. That's going to be the key for you, Victoria. If it was done maliciously, it will be bad for you. If it was not, it will be just a mistake that we all forget about."

Victoria watched his eyes. They were unreadable and cold. Suddenly, she felt a chill run down her spine.

"Since I'm leaving tomorrow, may I speak freely with you, then?" She breathed deeply. Her small breast pressed against her silk blouse.

Dmitry smiled. The full prominence of his jaw bone and his deep dimples emerged. His eyes sparkled. Licking his lips, he sat back in the chair with his long, muscular legs open.

"Talk," he said, giving her a sensual look. "Tell me what's on that mind of yours."

"I love your family. In the short time that I have worked for you, you all have grown to be very important to me."

Dmitry smiled but was silent.

"And I have to say, in watching Anya and how alone she is, I am very concerned. Mistress Medlov spends all of her time in a drunken haze or on pills…I've seen her take them…and I feel like you all deserve more."

"More?   How much more can one family have, Victoria?"

"Money doesn't solve every problem, sir."

"No?" Dmitry licked his lips. "I have yet to run across a problem that could not be solved by *the all mighty dollar*," he lied facetiously. If he had thought just once that his money would have saved his wife, he would be a happy poor man.

"I have a good relationship, Anya. I have a good relationship with your staff. Maybe you should reconsider sending me away? At this pivotal time in her young life, she needs stability. I can offer her that." She smile and leaned forward towards him, rubbing her hand across her breast as she did so. "I can offer *you* that, Dmitry." Her lips were wet, legs spread apart, heart racing, waiting for him to take her.

Dmitry sat back up, reached out and pulled her seat over to him in one quick movement. Her neck jerked. She was startled at his reaction and his raw strength. She inhaled his cologne as he looked her up and down.

"So you want to me to keep you on my staff?" he said cleverly. His voice was low and deep.

"Yes," she said, looking at his crotch. "I want to be on your *staff*, permanently."

Dmitry laughed. "So that's what this is all about. You want me to fuck you, *eh*?" He pulled her out of her seat and pulled her into his lap. She felt his erection.

"You are beautiful…tempting, but I'm not really into having a whore on staff. I despise whores, Victoria." His minty breath tickled her nose. He ran his large hand down her small back and circled her waist.

"I am *no* whore," she said defensively. "My feelings for you are genuine." She leaned into him, transfixed by his beautiful features and his strong body. "Is it wrong to want a man who has been forgotten by his wife, denied even? I only seek to offer you what she refuses."

Dmitry allowed her draw nearer. Inwardly, he fought the words that seem to resonate with the loneliness that he had felt for many years.

"Let me make you feel alive again." She leaned over into him, grabbed his chiseled face in her warm hands and kissed his soft, pink full lips.

It was a slow, wet kiss that seemed to go deeper with each motion. She could not get enough of the taste of his mouth, the smell of his cologne. He pulled her closer to his body, gripping her with both regret and need. His erection stabbed the bottom of her dress, pressed through her legs.

She moaned in torture. He was obscenely huge. She wanted him even more now. Her mouth watered at the prospect of him.

"Maybe you're right," Dmitry said, pulling away slowly.

His eyes opened and he tried to rationalize with himself. He pushed her off his lap roughly and then stood up. Walking over to the large mirror, he pulled her over to it and placed her in front of him. She could feel his erection still prodding at her from behind.

"Maybe you're not a whore, but you're definitely not a woman I can trust," he whispered.

"You can trust me more than you can trust *her*," Victoria said, aching to have him.

Dmitry's voice was low. "Let me look at you."

He ran his fingers down her body, along her solid frame.

"I want you," she said, feeling his hands on her body. "Take me."

"In my life, you can only be one of two things to me in the capacity that you are asking…my wife," he unzipped her skirt and pulled it off of her. "Or my whore." The skirt hit the floor, revealing black lace panties that showed her flawless frame. "Which is it, Victoria?" his mouth watered.

"Your wife," she whispered.

Dmitry smiled. "So that's it. You did this to replace her?"

"Yes," she said, unable to take his fondling.

"Well, to be my wife, you have to go through something of an initiation."

"Whatever, it takes," she closed her eyes and rested her head back on his abdomen. Her high was at its peak.

Dmitry's face was like stone as he looked at their reflection in the mirror. He reached behind him under his shirt and pulled a blade out. Holding it to her neck, he gripped her body. "First, I'll have to cut small slits into your body."

Her eyes opened. Startled, she winced and tried to get away. He put his hand over her mouth and bent to her ear. "Then, I'll have to strangle you until you know better than to scream."

Tears ran down her face.

"Then, I'll have to bend you over after I fuck you mercilessly and sodomize you until you bleed." His face was now dark. "But that's not it." He pulled her closer to the mirror. "Then, I have to cut your fucking throat. And then," he pulled her as she fought, "if you live, then after you've been mutilated and destroyed, then I can marry you." He licked the side of her face, just as he had heard Ivan had done to his wife.

She tried to scream, but she couldn't breathe. As she stared into the mirror, helpless to the mad man's strong hold, she saw tears in Dmitry's eyes. Anger and hatred painted over his face. She was suddenly paralyzed by fear.

"And you wonder why she's a bitch?" Dmitry smirked. "She used to be sweet, innocent, happy but not anymore…and it's all because of me. Does that turn you on? Huh? You like that? I'm sure that I could turn you into a shell of a woman, too. I could destroy every inch of you, too. And it wouldn't take me nearly as long as it did with her, you black-hearted bitch."

For a moment, Dmitry lost control. He had never had a desire to hurt any woman, but for what she was hiding, he wanted to hurt her now. Still there was that animalistic desire to have her beautiful body. The combination was lethal and caused the blood to course through his veins at a powerful speed. He felt as though he would have a heart attack, but still he did not stop his antics.

Desperately, she fought to get away, but he only gripped her down harder.

"Let go of me!" she screamed out. "You crazy bastard!"

"What? You don't want me now?" he taunted, disgusted by both Victoria and himself. "I thought that you wanted to *get married*."

"Help!" she screamed. "Someone help me!"

"Who's going to help you? You belong to me now."

"Let her go, Dmitry," Royal commanded from the shadows. Her voice was calm.

Dmitry looked up in the mirror with a wild devious look on his angelic face to see his wife.

Chapter 10

Royal could feel the heat seeping through her skin. Hearing the woman beg for her husband was a sobering reality check, but seeing her husband brutalize another woman was a repulsive reminder.

Earlier she had leaned against the door, hidden in the shadows, praying that the words that came from Dmitry would be true. Alas, they were. And while she was pained at his apparent attraction to Victoria, none could deny his disdain for her treachery.

Dmitry looked over at his wife instantly ashamed of his actions. He threw Victoria on the floor and slipped his knife back into the leather holder under his shirt.

How long had she been there in the dark? Did she see him kiss her? Did she see his steely erection? Could she hear in his voice his mild satisfaction with himself? He clenched his wide jaw and stilled himself where he stood, locking his body to ensure that he did not move from his place.

"Mrs. Medlov," Victoria said, standing up with her clothes pooled down around her ankles. "Thank you so much."

"*Thank you?*" Royal smirked.

She walked out of the shadows in a slow, cat-like sway. Her long dark hair busied itself around her body in an untamed, curly frame. Even in the same ruined clothes, she still mirrored absolute perfection.

Dmitry was only enraged more by the torn, tattered look of his wife. The click of her shoes stabbed the silence of the room and echoed about. The embers and light of the fireplace illuminated her dark features. He could not take his eyes off of her. It was if her presence diminished anyone else in the room, even himself.

"Victoria, I'm not the smartest woman in the world," Royal said softly. "But I'm willing to bet that you had something to do with my little *breakdown* earlier." Slowly, Royal walked over to the fireplace and pulled from the rack a black steel fire poker.

Victoria watched her mistress carefully. Breathing hard, she slipped on her dress as quickly as she could and looked back at Dmitry. His eyes were planted on Royal. It was as if his wife had cast a spell on him.

"I'm afraid that I don't know what you are talking about Mrs. Medlov," Victoria denied as she looked to Royal.

"What did you slip me?"

"Nothing."

"You know. I'm getting really tired of being the victim, Victoria. For too long, I've been the *injured party*. I won't let it happen again, not even one more time." Royal turned and walked towards her. "It will work out better for you if you just tell me the truth."

"Nothing," Victoria said adamantly. She looked her mistress in the eyes as they stood face-to-face. "I'm not responsible for what happened upstairs."

"What if I had died?" Royal continued in a calm voice as if the woman had not denied her treachery. "What if my heart had exploded?" They stood in the darkness only inches from each other. Royal gripped the fire poker in one hand as she stood erect.

"I don't know what you're talking about," Victoria said curtly. "You must be mistaken."

Royal made a step closer. The heat from the poker was only inches from both of them. "Sure you don't want to recount your *recollection*. My husband was already on the way to doing you bodily harm. I wouldn't want to finish the job for him."

"Oh, I'll finish it myself, love," Dmitry snarled.

Suddenly, she realized that if she were not completely honest she might never leave this room alive.

"Please don't," Victoria said quickly.

Royal's hand began to shake. "Then you tell me the truth, you lousy bitch! Did you slip me something in my drink?"

"Yes," Victoria said shaking. "Cocaine and Oxycotin. But I no idea you would end up the way that you did. I took some myself. It was just supposed to get you out of the way, not *harm* you."

Royal read her eyes. She knew that Victoria was telling the truth.

"I let you into my home, around my daughter and family. I let you drive our cars, dine at my table, and you repay me by trying to sleep my husband, take my family and kill me?"

Victoria could no longer look her in the eyes. "Forgive me, Mistress," she begged.

Royal's hand shook as she gripped the fire poker. Many thoughts crossed her mind. Thoughts of mutilation and retribution. But she knew that it was wrong. Finally, she opened her fingers and let the poker hit the ground.

"If there were not *just* one ounce of God of me, you'd be dead. I'd kill you myself." Tears ran down her face. "But there is…so…get out," Royal said barely above a whisper. "And don't *ever* let me lay eyes on you again, or so help me, I'll finish you." She looked over at Dmitry who stood in shock. "Davyd!" she screamed.

"Yes, Mistress," he said, opening the door quickly.

"Pack her in less than ten minutes and get her off my property. Do you understand?"

"Yes, Mistress," he said sternly as he watched the woman walk past him. He eyed Dmitry for more direction, but his boss's eyes were on his wife.

As the door closed, Dmitry breathed out slowly. The truth of Victoria's words were sobering and paralyzing in the same breath. The combination of drugs could have been fatal.

It took everything in him not to grab her by her small head and crack her spine, but his wife in his complete opposite had been so amazingly gracious until he felt ashamed.

Royal looked at him with a look of complete condescension. It was apparent to him without her saying one word that she had witnessed far more than he would have ever wanted her to see. Plus, he feared that the woman's lipstick and scent were upon him now. He could barely look at her, yet he could not keep his eyes from her.

Turning, she walked out of the room quietly down the hall. Dmitry followed behind her, unsure of where she was going. She went down the dark entryway towards the main hall, never looking back. When she got to the large double doors that led outside, she opened them and turned to Dmitry with tears in her eyes.

"All I want is a break through," she said sighing. "Is that so much to ask?"

"No," Dmitry said, uncomfortable for some reason.

"I don't suppose that you understand what the hell I'm talking about, do you?" She searched his face.

Dmitry was silent.

"I want to be free from it, Dmitry," she answered finally.

Rain blew in with the winds from the open door and wet the marble flooring and her body.

"Just tell me what you want me to do," Dmitry said in a soft voice.

He watched the rain drench the rugs and soak the floor. Normally that would have been enough to send her into a tirade, but she ignored it now.

"I want you to want me the way that you wanted that woman just a minute ago – so badly until it hurts," Royal confessed. "With passion," she smiled. Tears still fell.

"Royal, I do. I want you more."

Walking out into the rain, Royal headed down the steps of her home, unsure of where she was going. The water drenched her body, made her clothes stick. She walked off the concrete pathway to the lake about two hundred meters from the house.

Dmitry followed her; still unsure of what she was going to do.

The wind beat against her skin and stung her face as its wet beads slapped against it. Still, she kept walking, crying and talking to herself. In the grass, her long stilettos stabbed the dirt and mud. She fought through the mush and continued.

When she got to the lake, she leaned against a tall oak tree and sighed as she looked over the water. Running her hand over the cool wood, she saw her wedding ring sparkling in the night. Turning to see Dmitry standing behind her, she looked up at him with need.

"No matter what she says, she can't love you the way that I can," Royal assured.

"I would never let her."

"I'm not a *shell of woman*, Dmitry. I'm just try-ing to figure this all out."

"Let's figure it out together, please."

"Can we? Do you we really have what it takes to stay together?"

"I know that I don't have what it takes to stay apart from you and my family."

He pushed her long locks from her face, wiped the rain water from her lips and bent down to her kiss her. She grabbed his hot face and held it in her hands, rubbing through his stubby beard and caressing his skin. His eyes burned through her. They were filled with need and desperation. Slowly with growing passion, she began to kiss him deeper and deeper. As she did so, he dropped to his knees and pulled her close to him. His knees sank in the mud.

"She was right about one thing..."

"Shh..." Dmitry said, covering her lips. "Don't say a word."

Dmitry pulled at the strap of her slip with his cold, long fingers. It fell to her waist, revealing her full round breasts, erect and wet from the rain. He looked up at her and then kissed her burning nipples. He suckled her like a baby, wrapping his arms around her to draw her near in his embrace. Shuttering, she sucked in her breath in awe of what he promised.

She felt his large hands at her waist as he pulled down her slip, then her stockings, then at last her panties. Before she knew it, she was naked, standing before him both ashamed and aroused. She tried to cover her womanhood, but he her held her arms – needing to see all of her, scars and all.

Quickly, he took off his own clothes and laid them in the mud by the lake. She looked down at the ground amused. *Was he serious?* He laid her down carefully on his make shift bed and for the first time in her life, she felt cold mud and grass against her skin.

She expected to be turned off, to squeal and run, but the raw look of passion in Dmitry's eyes made her forget everything.

He bent down and kissed her as the rain beat against his body. Incredibly, he shielded her from most of its fury. She grabbed his neck as he ducked to her. He kissed her again. The passion so invigorating it sent deep chills down her spine.

Opening her legs, she felt his erect cock, warm and strong prodding between her steaming thighs. She bit her lip, arched her back and then slowly allowed him to enter her. The warm stiffness of his phallic pleasure electrified her.

To say it had been a while would have been an understatement. The bizarre and dynamic emotion that overwhelmed her brought tears to her eyes as he penetrated her.

It had been so long. It had been so needed. She closed her eyes and formed her lips into a pouty moue of ecstasy. She laid her head back in the dirt, forgetting her surroundings as he planted his knees in the earth and pushed into her body.

Her hands found their way to his waist as she tried to keep her sanity. His strokes were long, powerful and warm. It was such a dramatic contrast from their cold, wet surroundings. Reaching out for her, he grabbed the orb of her brown breasts with one hand and reached to hold on to her backside with the other. She felt her body lift off the ground, break apart in his hands. Letting out a moan, she began to shake, but he continued to stroke her, to fill her with every inch of himself.

She ran her hands over his now nearly shaven head and kissed him again, this time biting his bottom lip.

He rolled over and landed in the dirt with her on top now covered in black earth from her hair to her feet. She bent down and winced as she felt his entire throbbing penis inside of her. She tried to pull back to ease the pain, but he raised his aching thighs and pushed as far as he could.

Her mouth parted in rapture. Dmitry gave a slow, wicked grin. Kissing her breasts, he moved below her slowly, breaking all the barriers that had been placed between them. Her cheeks reddened with fire. She began to shiver out of control. Leaning over, she grabbed the grass and pulled it as he made love to her.

It pleased him immensely to watch her finally come alive. Her mouth opened in awe in pleasure and pain. She moaned aloud, moving faster against him, slicking their bodies with her wetness. His strokes were wet and long, deep and hard. It was a passion that could not be given by money, by the love a child, by power. It was something that could only be shared by lovers. Suddenly, she felt the apex of her pleasure approaching. Her body began to throb and ache. She looked down at him in wonderment as her body began to vibrate on its own. It shook uncontrollably.

Ferociously, his pleasure caused her back to spasm, her hands to clinch, her eyes to roll. She called out his name as she did. How could a man make a woman feel this beautiful? As she orgasmed for the first time in nearly a year, the rain stopped. Only the cool wind beat against them.

"I love you," she said with tears in her eyes.

"I love you, too," he said, biting his lip. "But I can't hold it any longer?" His breathing became sporadic. His skin was beat red.

"It's not safe. I'm not on the pill." She tried to pull away.

There was a strange look in his eyes. "So, if I didn't pull out, we could get pregnant?"

"Yes. *Sheesh*. We sound like teenagers," she laughed.

Dmitry didn't laugh. "Let me."

Royal looked at him thoughtfully.

A shock went through him as his body pleaded to release inside of her.

"Who cares that you're not on pill; let me. Like before Anya, before Ivan." He pushed inside of her again. "Let me remember what it feels like to have my wife."

Tears ran down her face. She shook her head.

"How in the hell do you do that, Dmitry?"

"Do what?"

"Change my entire life in seconds," she whispered. "A few minutes ago I wanted to die."

"And now?"

"And now, I have never felt so alive."

Dmitry pulled her lips to his and kissed her as his skin began to burn and clamor. He pushed slowly into her body, more erect that ever. His muscles tightened as he felt the silk from her body on his own.

The mere knowledge of the intimate transaction that was about to take place aroused him more. He rested his nearly clean-shaven head back and felt the cool ground against it.

Royal looked down at his muscular body tensed up and bulging below her. His eyes sparkled in the darkness, guiding her thoughts in the black of the night.

Suddenly, she felt a powerful pulse inside of her. It had been so long since she allowed him to do so, so long since he had asked. But the feeling was joyous. It was a remarkable sensation that only a woman could have, a pleasure that only a wife could imagine. The possibility of life. The certainty of love.

Chapter 11

The cold fierce winds finally brought the reunited couple back to reality and sent them running from the lake back to the front doors of their home, where they had started their journey a full hour before.

Dmitry opened the unlocked door slowly with Royal on his back laughing and naked, covered from head to toe in dirt. They entered the house talking loudly and giggling like school kids.

The doctor that Dmitry had sent for earlier stood with his assistant and Davyd in the foyer looking on mortified at the sight of the exposed couple.

"Dmitry, we have guests," Royal blushed. She hid her breasts on his back.

"Oh, hello, Doc."

Dmitry didn't bother to cover himself, but he did make sure not to turn where they could see Royal's rear end as she clung to his back like a Koala bear.

"Hello, Mr. Medlov," Dr. Finlen said, trying to look away from the massive dirty giant. "You remember my assistant, Kyle," the doctor motioned over at the young man staring with his mouth wide open at the spectacle.

"Yes, I remember him," Dmitry said, reaching his hand out then quickly retracting it. "Sorry. I'll shake your hand later. I'm just a little…"

"Indisposed at the moment," Royal finished.

"So which one of you am I supposed to be here to treat?" the doctor asked with a grin. "Both of you appear a little unstable right now."

"Neither. It appears that I had her cure all along," Dmitry smirked.

"Well, what was the problem, if you don't mind me asking? It sounded urgent on the phone when Davyd called."

"I was slipped cocaine and Oxycotin, doctor," Royal answered.

"Oh my goodness! By whom?" Dr. Finlen was very concerned having known for many years the Royal's fragile state.

"The teacher," Royal answered. "She confessed."

"What?" Davyd's outburst showed his shock. He looked over at Royal with a furrowed brow. She had been drugged under his nose!

Dmitry smiled. "I wish that you had known when I asked you to put her out, Davyd. Your anger might have taught her a lesson more astringent than Royal's."

"Where is the woman?" Dr. Finlen asked.

"I don't know," Dmitry looked to Davyd for an answer.

"I had one of the security guards take her to Prague and drop her off in city. She was told to find her own way home and to be out of country by noon tomorrow."

"Well, it's a Friday night. I'm sure if she works hard enough by morning she'll have enough money for an airline ticket," Dmitry smirked.

Royal hit him and laughed. The infectious and untimely happiness of the couple made everyone snicker, including Stepan, who appeared from nowhere with two robes.

"Thank you," Dmitry reached out quickly for the robes. "Why don't you take our guests to the sitting room, and Royal and I will be down in just a minute, Stepan."

"Yes, sir," he said quickly.

Davyd shook his head and followed Stepan and the guests into the west wing of the house.

Alone again, Dmitry set Royal on the floor and dressed her in the pink fluffy robe. Pulling her curly hair from her face, he bit his lip.

"Well that was embarrassing," she said, closing his robe around his waist and tying it. "Now everyone has seen what all the fuss is about."

Dmitry laughed and put his hands on her arms. "Well, it is a pretty big *fuss*. You know...we should probably go upstairs and get into something more appropriate before we go in there and talk to them, *eh*?"

Royal bit her lip. "I know what you're trying to do, Dmitry." She grinned and looked down at the marble floor.

Dmitry raised his brows and smiled, revealing his dimples. "What? I just want to make sure we don't continue to make scene. Did you see that poor kid? He couldn't keep his eyes off you."

"Hush," Royal bit out, laughing. "They are going to hear you."

"They can't hear me." He pulled her to him. "Let's go upstairs for…twenty minutes."

"No, that's too long."

"Ten minutes?"

"No, Dr. Finlen got up and came out here in the middle of the night. He's exhausted and very old. We can't make him wait."

"He can spend the night. We have a thousand bedrooms."

"No."

"Five minutes?" he bargained, licking his lips. He growled and pulled her to him. "If you say no again, I'll take you right here in the middle of the floor."

Royal paused. "Fine. Five minutes is all you get and that includes the time it takes to get dressed." She giggled.

"Well, I better start on the way up there," he said, opening his robe jokingly.

***

The sun crept into Anatoly's suite and cast a glow over his naked body as he lay awake thinking. His father had left the night before suddenly an unexplained, which left him assuming it had something to do with Royal.

He was still perplexed by their ever-evolving relationship of trial after trial, and it plagued him why his father had left a lifestyle as opulent as theirs to be with one woman.

What could one woman provide? He had never known one worth the trouble. Each he had met had a sob story that reeked of neediness and fragility that he could neither identify with nor stomach.

But he did love Anya. The fruit of his father and step mother's toils was a blooming girl whom he loved past words. Yet, he was certain that one could have a child without marriage. It had been done in his family for many generations.

There had been no father there to guide him until he sought out Dmitry. And while he did not wish his life on his little sister, he also did not wish a life of constant bickering between parents who had everything and still chose to fight about the nothingness in a relationship.

His cell phone rang, pulling him from his thoughts of his checkered past into the present. He reached over past the young blonde beside him and grabbed his cell. The number was unknown. Odd. He answered hesitantly.

"Hello," he said, sitting up in the bed.

"Mr. Medlov," a woman with a Russian accent said coolly. "We are interested in your offer."

"Good," Anatoly held his sigh of relief. "I assume that there are terms." He recognized her voice as the liaison on the yacht the night before.

"Yes. We will be getting back with you on that in the next twenty-four hours. Until then, we ask that you keep your phone on."

"Of course," Anatoly answered, feeling the young woman stir beside him.

He hung up his phone and smiled. His father would be pleased that things had worked out. This would mean a new era for the Medlov family and new power for him that he had been hungry for now for over three years.

"Excuse me, miss," he nudged the woman.

"Yes," her eyes opened to full intense brown beams.

He was certain that she was probably awake the entire time, lingering beside him to the bitter end as women often did the morning after.

"It's time for you to go," he said gently. "Get your things, and I'll have a car take you to your place." Rubbing her arm, he watched her obediently pull her body from the bed and begin to get dressed.

***

Dorian's assistant hung up the phone and looked over at him. He sat eagerly on the end of his desk pealing an apple and listening to the short conversation.

He nodded at her and looked at his laptop. From his assistant's report of the bids, the Medlov family was short a guest by the end of the night.

He had never expected them to show but was glad that they did. He had unfinished business with Dmitry and would use the opportunity to end their war one way or another.

Dmitry had slaughtered his friend, Ivan, three years ago. It had been a bloody, brutal battle in the streets of Memphis and at the Medlov compound.

His only regret, the thing that haunted him nightly, was the rape and murder of a young woman who was an innocent.

The pictures of her under surveillance were burned into his mind forever.

Royal was a beautiful black woman with promise and compassion. Plus, the most horrible of the reports on her death was that she was with child. *A double sin.* Her end was undeserved, but it was Dmitry who had helped them all bring her to it.

Dorian thought because of his own involvement, God would have been angry with him and punished him with death or at least poverty. But he had prospered beyond belief after the bombings, all without Dmitry knowing or pursuing him.

However, the fact that Dmitry had shown up at the bid last night meant that he was back. The rumors of his retirement had to have been false. And with a man as powerful as Dmitry Medlov calling the shots through his son and revenge still on his brain for his dead fiancé and child, there would be little to no refuge for him now.

"Find out where the boy is going," Dorian ordered the woman. "Find out where he lives, where Dmitry lives and how to get close to him. Then report back to me. I'll go there myself."

"Yes, sir," the tall blonde said, getting up from the desk to leave her boss alone to think and plan.

The Medlov bid had come in 30% higher than everyone else's. That was their typical style. Anything that they wanted, they got.

This shipment was a once-in-a-lifetime opportunity and it had to be handled with the utmost care.   His clients would never turn down the lucrative Medlov offer; he was certain of it.

But he was responsible for the handling of the bids, the logistical transfer of goods and money and the final meeting for payment, which meant that he and Dmitry would have to come in contact with each other at some point. The tide would surely turn then for both of them once Boss Medlov realized who he was dealing with regardless of its lucrative nature.

Dorian considered the Intel a leg up in the situation. If he could find out everything before Dmitry knew anything at all, he could make the deal for his clients and wipe out his nemesis all at the same time.

The word on Anatoly was that he was Dmitry's son. He had no quarrels with him and therefore planned to leave him unharmed. He would come out of this the most powerful gunner runner in the world and one family member short. No one would ever know who had done it. And his revenge for both his friend, Ivan, and his need to be rid of his most dangerous enemy would be over.

Chapter 12

Midmorning came and went and Royal and Dmitry were still holed up in their bedroom. Brigitte had knocked early that morning with breakfast for the pair and found the Medlov's were occupied. The word through the grapevine in the house was that they had rekindled their love naked in the rain and mud by the lake after a brief shoot out on the second floor in the family quarters.

Evidently one of the lawn workers, who lived in the quarters behind the house, had seen them rolling around on the ground screwing like wild animals. It had also been confirmed by the workers that Dmitry was hung like a horse. Brigitte smiled to herself. *So was Anatoly for that matter.* It must haven been a family trait.

"We should probably get up," Royal said, raising her head off of Dmitry's chest. Their bodies were sweaty and exhausted from hours of love making.

"I'm starving," Dmitry said, picking her up and pulling her closer to him. "What do you want to eat? I call chef."

"I don't know," she yawned and stretched. "Eggs, bacon, pancakes with strawberries, orange juice, grits and a side of honey butter."

"Shit," Dmitry scoffed.   "I need paper to write all that down."

"Well, it's been a long night," she explained.

"I think I pulled my hamstring," Dmitry grabbed his leg.

"Yeah, well, I'm certain I pulled my back. Try having a 300-pound man pummel you from behind sometimes."

"No, thank you," he smiled. Dmitry tapped her exposed backside and pulled himself from her body.   "I could still go another round," he said, standing on the side of the bed stretching.

"Later," Royal smiled.   "Right now, I want to see Anya."

"I texted Davyd earlier.   He said that she was still sleeping.   Last night was very scary for her."

"I know," Royal stopped smiling.   "We owe her an explanation.   She probably thinks that I'm crazy, Dmitry."

"Nonsense.   Anya loves you.   She knows that you would never do anything to harm her.   If it makes you feel better, we give her a talking to together when she wakes up.   Maybe make up with her with the borscht she likes for papa to cook?   I do it myself after shower.   Make big meal."

"That sounds good, but I still want breakfast."

"I know. I know. I get you breakfast. You get all the energy you can, because we do this all again this evening."

"Maybe we can leave out the cocaine and guns this time around."

"Hey, it spiced it up a little," he joked with her.

There was a hard knock on the door. Everyone knew not to bother them. Who could be that insolent?

Royal covered up while Dmitry walked over to the door. He opened it just a little and looked down. It was Anatoly.

"Papa. I just got home. Davyd told me what happened to Royal and Anya. Is Royal alright?"

Dmitry looked back at Royal, who was sitting up in the bed. "It's Anatoly," he said, calming her. "I'll be back."

Grabbing the robe off the ground, he wrapped it around his body and stepped outside. His son looked up at him angrily awaiting an explanation on what had happened to Anya.

"Everyone is fine, Anatoly," Dmitry assured as he walked with him down the hallway.

"Well, what did you do to the bitch?" Anatoly asked fuming.

"I wanted to do *something*, but Royal insisted that she just leave." Even Dmitry was dumbfounded. "Her father will surely be put off the payroll, and I'll give her a scathing report."

"*Report?* You've gone soft," Anatoly snapped.

"Well, what would you have me to do, *oh great little one?*" Dmitry clenched his jaw.

"Nothing," he shook his head and remembered his place. "I came home to tell you about deal. I got call this morning like you said I would. I headed here straight afterwards."

Dmitry smiled. He was proud of his son. "Good. Now you just wait for instruction. I assume you have plan for transportation, warehousing and distribution of all these weapons?"

"*Da*, but I won't need it for long. I have struck deal with a Jewish group outside of Palestine. Most of them are headed straight there as soon as order is final."

"You are getting around, aren't' you?"

"I told you that I'd make you proud."

"And you have," he said, opening Anya's door as they stopped. He looked in quickly on his little one. Her curtains had been drawn, and she slept peacefully in her bed with her bunny rabbit.

The sight calmed his spirits. He was forced to smile. Anatoly stuck his head in also. He scanned the room and sighed. He didn't know what he would do if something ever happened to Anya. Neither of them did. She was their solace.

They both closed the door and continued downstairs without speaking anymore about her.

"Are you going to change to clothes?" Anatoly asked.

"*Da*, I just needed to get Royal some breakfast and tell the cook to make sure that I have what I need to fix meal for Anya before she wakes up."

"You cooking borscht?" Anatoly asked.

"Yes."

"Fix enough for me." His eyes were bright.

"I cook for entire family today, as sort of a celebration."

"Of what?"

"Reconciliation," Dmitry joked.

Anatoly smirked. "It sounds odd coming from a man who can literally have any woman that he wants or *doesn't want*. Davyd told me what happened last night between you and Victoria. I told you that you couldn't trust her."

"You did. And I didn't trust her. I ignored her, which is just as bad, I suppose. Look what happened. I nearly lost my wife last night," he shook his head.

Anatoly's face reddened with anger, but he tried to hide it. He interrupted his father. "Well, look, I have to run into town for minute. When I come back, let's talk about the deal and have dinner as family," Anatoly said, headed for the car garage.

"How long will you be gone?" Dmitry asked, standing the in foyer in his robe as the maids scurried past him with naughty grins. "I start cooking in about an hour."

"Not long, papa." Anatoly turned and walked away. "Close your robe all the way. The maids are looking."

***

Victoria settled down at a small restaurant in the square not far from the airport to eat before she headed up to her hotel room for a while to rest.

She had found a flight out of Prague for the following morning and planned to leave this place for good. Of course Davyd had told her to be out of Prague by noon, but it wasn't like he could do anything to her now that she had left the *animal farm*. Plus, it was already going on 1:30, and she was starving.

Her plan had hardly turned out in her favor. She was humiliated by that undercover psycho, Dmitry, threatened by his dizzy wife, kicked out by the grandpa of the house without even being able to collect all of her belongings and forced to ride in a Smart Car back to the city with a very smelly security guard, who looked at her legs the entire thirty-minute drive. He had dropped her

22

in the center of town, thrown out her bags and pulled off in the rain.

In another humiliating move, she had to call her father and beg him to purchase her a ticket on her behalf. He had immediately inquired about the termination instead of asking if she was alright.

Of course, she had avoided telling him that she had drugged the mistress with a cocktail that could have easily killed her and propositioned Dmitry while his wife was tripping. She omitted that she had been dragged from the house by her arm and thrown out in the courtyard – made to wait on the smelly security guard. She definitely avoided telling him that she herself was high on cocaine – even though he knew about her *problem*.

She only said that it had not worked out and the Medlov's where no longer in need of her services. She would tell him more of the truth when she was back in DC and away from this place.

***

Anatoly shifted gears and tore through the streets of Prague on his cell phone. One of his contacts said that he had spotted Victoria at a restaurant in Prague 1.

If he rushed, he could get to her and deal with the bitch himself. How could his father just allow her to leave unharmed? How could Royal allow her to leave after all that had happened to her? He shook his head in disgust.

Soft. Stupid. The both of them were. They had gotten so wrapped up in their little fairy tale until they couldn't even deal with reality anymore.

He hadn't figured out what he would do just yet, but he figured that an eye for an eye would just about make them even. It had to be done for Anya if for no one else. He pulled up to the front of his father's restaurant, where a young man stood waiting.

As soon as he saw Anatoly, he ran over to the car.

"Boss, you want us to take of? This is small shit. One of us can do it. I can do it. It would be honor," he said in a Russian accent, leaning over into the window of Anatoly's car.

"No, it's personal. I'll take care of it. You got my shit?"

"*Da,*" he handed Anatoly a small vile. "It was just made...for you."

"For her," Anatoly said nodding. "She's still eating?"

"Over at the Plzeňská restaurant at Municipal House. She's eating outside."

"*Spasibo, brat,*" Anatoly said, speeding off.

The sun gleamed through his curly strands of hair as the wind ripped through the windows of his Bentley. Someone could have mistaken the young man for a model or an actor, but Anatoly was what he was. A killer. The thought of the act of killing her itched through him now. He wanted to peel the skin from her bones for the blatant disrespect she had shown his family.

However, he wasn't sure exactly what he was going to do to her. He would play it by ear. Pulling quickly on to Republiky, he parked outside of the Municipal House and slipped on his Aviator shades.

People were out in droves. Tourist stood outside taking pictures and laughing in the square. Business people walked up and down Republiky Street pasted to their cell phones as small taxi cabs sped by.

Anatoly couldn't blend. His splendor stood out among the crowd. Women watched him as he passed, eyed him as he approached. He was his father's son. Beautiful.

Clutching his keys in his hands, he walked down the sidewalk to the tables lined up on the walkway outside the building and found Victoria there eating with her back turned from him. He smiled a little. From afar, she seemed harmless. Attractive.

A waitress batted her eyes at him as he sailed by with a cool swagger that hid his inner rage. He licked his lips and slid into the chair across from her abruptly, startling her on purpose.

"You should have taken Davyd's advice and left Prague before noon," he said with a clever smile. He revealed the deep dimple in his left cheek. "Instead you lunch like you're on fucking vacation."

Victoria looked up stunned. "Anatoly? What are you doing here? What happened to your hair?" She put down her fork and wiped her face with her napkin.

"I was looking for you," his deep baritone voice carried. He ignored her second question.

"Why?" her heart stopped.

"Unfinished business," he raised his eyebrows. "You have been very bad girl, Victoria."

She looked into his eyes and saw the malice. Instantly, she stood up to leave, but he grabbed her wrist and yanked her back down to the table.

"Where you going?" his jaw clenched. "Don't make scene. It's not nice."

She sat back down and looked around. No one had seen her. She wanted to scream out, but fear gripped her.

"Mistress Medlov told me to leave. I left. It's finished now," she explained in a hushed tone. "I don't know what you want with me, but..."

Anatoly let go of her arm and pulled her drink over to him. "What is this?" he looked down in the glass.

"Wine," she felt her bruised wrist. Running her soft fingers over her delicate skin, she rolled her eyes at him.

"Chardonnay? What year?" He reached into his pocket and pulled out a vile.

She watched him as he opened it and dropped the white contents into the glass, then swirled it around. He pushed it back over to her and motioned for her to drink it.

"I'm doing you the courtesy of not sneaking it to you like fucking snake. Now drink it."

Tears ran down her eyes. "No."

"Drink ."

"No!" she snapped.

He reached across the table to her face. She shrieked away but felt his cold hand wipe the tear from her cheek.

"Drink it," he said softly with a soothing look in his eyes. She heard the gun click under the table. "Drink it...or else."

With shaking hands, she picked the glass up and put it to her pouty lips. Then finally while looking into his cold eyes, she drank it.

He put his index finger on the bottom of the glass and pushed to make sure that she drank all the contents. Then, he took the glass from her, checked the bottom of it and stood up.

She flinched, scared of what he might do to her. This was all supposed to be over. She had learned her lesson. She was out of a job, receiving a poor review and headed home – flat busted broke. She had spent most of her money on blow and shopping. What else did he want from her?

Looking down at the table, she wondered what she had just ingested. Cocaine? Oxycotin? Maybe something worse? Poison?

He stood beside her and tapped the table as he stared at the crown of her head.

"Alright, let's go," he said, grabbing her by her arm. He threw down money on the table and picked up her bags.

"Where are you taking me?" she asked struggling. Her tips toes brushed the ground as he nearly lifted her from it. "Let go of me!"

People looked at the odd couple as they made their way to his car. Anatoly never uttered a word, but without much of a struggle, he guided her roughly to the car.

"Get in." After throwing her inside, he slammed the door behind her, put her bags in the trunk and pulled off into the streets.

Victoria began to feel the heat rise from her stomach up into her chest. She laid her head back on the white leather seat and looked out of the window as they passed through the city at warp speed.

"Where are you taking me, you son of a bitch?" Her speech had already begun to slur.

"Somewhere *quiet*," he answered, focused on the road.

Flashes of light and dizziness overtook her. "Are you going to rape me?" she asked with tears in her eyes. "That's such a fucked up thing to do."

"Don't flatter yourself," he smirked. "I'm not animal. Well, not that kind of animal."

"Are you going to kill me then?" A warm sensation started to rip through her veins.

"I don't know. Do you deserve to die?"

"No," she whispered. "Pull this car over and let me go," she tried to open the door, even as Anatoly sped through the streets.

He hit the lock button and looked over at her. "Don't try anything stupid with me. I'm not my father. I'll speed up and throw your ass out when we cross the bridge. They won't find you until next week."

She swallowed hard and removed her hand from the door. It felt as if they were moving at the speed of light. And the growl in his voice made her believe him. No. She wouldn't test him. She feared him.

They pulled quickly into a gated community, a private drive and then into the garage of a large, modern condo. The garage door closed, and the dark space lit up.

Anatoly unlocked the doors and went quickly over to her side to the help her out. As he opened the door of the car, she nearly fell down. He grabbed her firmly, and she landed on his chest. Looking up at him, she lost herself in his eyes.

He was more beautiful than she remembered. His muscles were rock hard under his shirt, his cologne tantalizing like his father's, his eyes a strange deep blue, his perfectly chiseled square jaw clinched and his wide full mouth was only inches from hers. He watched her under thick lashes that flapped like wings. She couldn't tell if he was angry or crazy. His eyes had no depth to them.

"You're stumbling. Can you feel it yet?" he asked, grabbing her by her arm and yanking her around the car and up the concrete stairs to a door.

"Yes," she said, nearly falling over again.

There was something strange about the man. While there was obvious impending danger for her, she felt a reserve on his part, like he might be attracted to her, concerned about harming her. However, she couldn't be sure, hence the fear.

Whatever he had made her drink continued to blur her vision more. Grabbing the railing, she tucked her head and took a deep breath. Before she could rest her racing heart, he caught her by her waist and helped her up the stairs. She felt his groin on her butt, but he was not aroused, just focused.

Hitting a code on the alarm next to the door, he opened it and pulled her inside.

She looked around confused. This was a house. His house? He set his keys on the counter and motioned for her to follow him. She did so hesitantly.

The clicks of her heals tapped against the walnut woods floors as she slowly moved through the large space to a sitting room where she fell back against the couch.

Anatoly looked over at her drunken state and smirked. He stood looking out the window with his fists in his pockets.

She watched his muscular back filling out his cotton shirt from his broad shoulders to his long torso to the nice fitting jeans that outlined the muscular curve of his body. He finally turned around and looked at her.

"Do you know who we are?" he asked.

Her eyes fluttered. "You're the Medlov's."

"But do you know *who* we are?"

"No."

"Do you know what we do?"

"No."

He sucked in his breath and pulled his hands out of his pockets.

"You really should not have fucked with my stepmother."

"I know," she looked around the room. It was starting to get dim. "I said I was sorry. What is it with you people and theatrics?"

"What do you think I ought to do with you?"

"I don't know," she snapped.

"Here the thing. I don't know which one of the two options that I have to use. I did at first but not now. So, I'm asking your opinion. What do *you think* that *I* should do with *you*?"

"I've had a knife pulled on me, a poker shoved at me. I've been kicked out in the rain, drugged and kidnapped," she shook her head. "What else can be done? I'm really getting tired of this shit. So, do want you want to and stop fucking around with me already."

Anatoly paused for a minute. He liked her fight at least, but she needed to be taught a lesson for crossing the line. Plus, he wanted to see how far she could be pushed.

"Alright," he said, bending down.

She followed him with her eyes.

He raised his pants leg slightly and pulled out his gun. Cocking it, he pointed it at her.

She looked on speechless. Maybe she should not have spoken so quickly. The breath in her lungs caught in her throat, and the tears began to form. She clinched the pillows beside her and sat silent awaiting the shot.

Anatoly raised his brow, clicked off the safety and pulled the trigger three times. The silencer kept the noise down, but it didn't matter. The room was nearly sound proof, which was why he had led her there.

One shot. Two shots. Three shots. Bullets raced from the gun. The power of the small weapon was steadied in his hand.

Planted against the back of the couch, her eyes peered at him, unblinking and desperate. She finally took a breath, finally let go of the pillows, finally let the tears fall down her cheeks.

She was still alive. The bullets had barely missed her, rang into the wall removing chunks of drywall, leaving plugs in a three-point crown around her head.

"Now, do you want to continue to talk to me like that or do you want to live, *eh*?" he lowered his gun and waited for her give a smart reply. There was none.

"I want to live," she whispered.

Anatoly took a seat across the room from her and laid the gun on the table beside him. He respected that she hadn't screamed, respected that she hadn't begged. He did like her, even though he hated himself for it. He liked her when he first laid eyes on her. Liked her when he saw her around the house. Liked her when he left his father's today headed to kidnap her. Liked her in her perfect little outfit with her perfect little deep chocolate features.

Needless to say, Royal would be pissed, but there was something about Victoria that he found to be interesting – interesting enough not to kill yet and interesting enough to utilize.

"You should be disoriented enough that you won't remember how to get back here. If you aren't that disoriented, you still don't bring your ass back here. You understand?"

"Yes."

"Alright. This is how it's going to be for you, Victoria. You need job, you need to get out of city safe, and you're trouble with my family, which means you're as good as dead. My father would have nothing to do with you, but I see your purpose, even if they don't."

"My purpose?"

Anatoly ignored her. "You plan to do back to D.C. tomorrow, today?"

"Yes. Tomorrow."

"Cancel. You're going to Memphis with me along with a few other stops. You're in my debt now, because I didn't slice your throat or sell you to dealer the way that you deserve. You're going to do some business for me, and you'll do it until

I tell you otherwise." He pointed her as he talked, eyeing her with a menacing glare.

"Like I told your father. I'm not some fucking whore," she said, scared but still unwilling to back down.

"Relax. Like I told you. I'm an animal, but I'm not that kind. Plus, you were willing to be whore less than a day ago. Humping on my father's leg like a grubby little bitch. Why are so sensitive now?"

"You jealous? Look, okay, I had the hots for your father. Get over it. There were a hundred before him. It wasn't about his looks, although it helped. It was about money. I'm sure you understand that concept though. Mistress Medlov seemed uninterested. I thought it would be easy. I fucked up. Obviously. Look at where I am. So what do you want from me now?"

"I need you to facilitate some things that you will be required to put your name on, some deals to be made. No one will suspect you. You're a nobody."

She ignored his snide remark. "Illegal business?"

"Is there any other kind?" he clinched his jaw. "You could be...should be dead right now, but I'm offering you opportunity to better yourself."

"It doesn't appear that I have much of a choice, do I tough guy? What makes you think that I won't go to the police though? And how do I know that you're not just setting me up to go jail?"

"I hate fucking pigs, so you won't have any dealings with them from me. And if you turn me in, I'll go to DC and visit your nice family and kill them deader than I'd kill you. And there's not a damn thing anyone can do about it, but you already know that, don't you?"

The threat hardly bothered Victoria. What did she give a damn about her family for? It had taken an act of God for them to pay for her ticket home. Screw them all. The immediate concern for her was money, not to mention that she hated cops too.

"I want the same rate of pay...no...I want double what your father was going to pay me. It sounds like you need me as much as I need you. And when I'm out of your debt, I want to walk away free and clear. None of this in-for-life servitude bullshit that you Russians are into. I've watched the movies. I know that those tattoos mean something very fucked up."

"If you were smart, you would have done your homework before you came here." He paused. "What makes you think I want you for life? Did I ask you to marry me? What are you, crazy?" Anatoly huffed. "You don't even know what you'll be doing yet, and you're already talking deal for double? I *should* put bullet in your head."

"Fine. Triple it."

She sat up on the couch a little straighter and moved her long dark hair from her face. Strands had fallen out of her neat ponytail during the struggle and now were wistfully. She looked like an angel.

It was hard for Anatoly to pay attention. She was beautiful; he would give her that. But she also was heartless and greedy. Those were two things that if used properly could help him once the deal in Sochi came through. He raised his brow.

"You mind if I smoke? My folks don't like it. Plus, it's not good example for little Anya."

"Knock yourself out," she shrugged.

He took out a silver case and pulled out a long slender cigarette. Sliding the tobacco between his full lips, he pulled out a lighter and lit it.

After taking a drag, he looked over at her and sat back in his seat with his legs open. Victoria instantly thought of his father. Sexy. Dangerously sexy men. She wondered what Anatoly was like in bed.

Anatoly watched her carefully. He knew what she was thinking. He could almost read her filthy mind word for word.

"I'll pay you what he agreed to pay you plus half. You stay where I tell you to stay. You do what I tell you to do. But if you talk to police or try to fuck me over, I kill you. Don't ever forget that and don't ever doubt me." His voice was low and calm but full of venom.

"I don't doubt you, but don't think that I fear you either," she lied. "This is a business arrangement. I'm not a whore, and I'm not fucking push over. I want double."

He almost laughed, but he didn't say no. He wouldn't because he planned to give her double.

"Double," she said again fading.

"There's no guarantee that my stepmother won't still kill you when she comes to her senses."

"If she didn't kill me then, she won't later."

"Don't be sure of yourself. Why...why my father?"

"You mean, why not you?"

"Yeah?"

"Because he seems mellow. You seem out of control, and I don't even know you."

"My father mellow? You are stupid."

"Yeah, I know that now. He pulled a blade and put it to my neck, then started choking me and crying and shit. Said something about sodomizing me and cutting me up. He's really fucked in the head. I thought he was going to rip me to shreds. Your stepmother actually saved me. He was always the calmer of the two, it seemed. Evidently, it was just a cover."

"Looks are deceiving," Anatoly smirked. He was proud of his father. She deserved it.

"What did you give me?" her heart pounded loudly. It felt as though it would pop out of her chest. She began to skip breaths. Her eyes rolled and hands clamored.

"You should be afraid to fall asleep around me," Anatoly said tauntingly. "You should afraid of where you'll wake up."

"As long as it's not in bed with you, I'll be fine."

"Bitch," he puffed blowing out a plume of smoke. "Still talking crazy even after all of that. You're just as fucked up as I am."

Victoria leaned back on the couch and closed her eyes. The drugs had settled in now. She began to drift off.

Anatoly watched her from across the room. From his view, he could see up her skirt to her red panties. Red was his favorite color. He looked away from her and bit his lip. His father was an idiot to pass up on her.

After finishing his cigarette, he walked over to the couch and leaned over her still body. She didn't flinch. He put his hand on her neck and checked her pulse, thought about strangling her and about screwing her.

It was apparent that she was going to be trouble, yet she made his heart race more than any woman he had ever met. Finally after a minute or two of deliberation, he reached down and picked her up.

Carrying her limp body through the large condo in his arms, he took her up the stairs to the master bedroom and laid her in the bed. He pulled her shoes off, examined her pedicure. Why? He didn't know. Then he went downstairs, rummaged through her well-organized purse to find her cell phone, ID and money, took it all and left the undisclosed place quietly.

Chapter 13

The mood at the Medlov Chateau was festive by dusk. The help dashed around the house in a cheery mood, filling it with blooming white, yellow and red roses, spraying perfumes, lighting candles, opening curtains and cleaning. It was as if the house had finally come alive after many years of lying dormant.

The night sky was accented by hues of red and gold as the sun set under a full moon and eager bright stars. The breathtaking view made the chateau look majestic. Surrounded by beautiful landscaping, a well-cut immaculate lawn that stretched on flat lands for miles, a sparking lake and beautiful weather, it appeared that there was no more beautiful place in the world.

Anatoly pulled onto the private drive and could see the home lit up a mile away. It appeared that everyone light in the house was on, every window open; even the lanterns leading down the drive had been lit. Alas, his father and stepmother were in a good mood. He pulled into the circular drive, hearing the gravel crush under this tires, jumped out and ran up the long steps to the front of the house. Stepan opened the door as he grabbed the knob and let him in.

"What's going on in here?" Anatoly asked, wiping his feet off on the rug.

"Your father says tonight he cooks for the entire house, staff, family and all. We're going to have dinner in the main hall."

"He hasn't done that since they moved in," Anatoly smirked. "And Royal?"

"She has the maids cleaning and then rushing to put on regular clothes to enjoy the evening. A band from in town is coming in an hour to set up and play music, and there is a rumor that Dmitry will announce a raise tonight for all workers."

"Wow. It's amazing what a little ass can do."

Stepan gave him a frown. It was completely inappropriate to speak of Mistress Medlov in that way. He shook his head at Anatoly, giving him a look of complete admonishment, yet the boy did not take offense to the old man's rigid manners.

"Lighten up, old man. I'm just kidding with you. Plus, you know it's true."

Cracking a grin, Anatoly hit the butler on the back and headed towards the kitchen where his father surely was.

There were Old World Russian recipe aromas filling the corridors. The pots clanged louder as he got closer to the kitchen. Opening the large double doors to the massive kitchen, he smiled at his father.

Dmitry looked different now, nearly bald with all of his beautiful hair cut off, but he still managed to look stately.

He looked up at his son and smiled. "I was wondering what you were up to," Dmitry waved him over to the stove. "Here, stir this while I check on my bread," he said, wiping his hands on his white apron.

"I heard that we are throwing party tonight," Anatoly said, stirring his father's legendary borscht.

"*Da*, we have huge Medlov-style dinner in main hall in about…" he checked his watch. "An hour."

"Why?"

"Why not?" he snapped.

"You're happy now, huh? Now that you have everything." Anatoly took the large wooden spoon from the pot and tasted the borscht.

Dmitry pulled the bread from the oven and placed it on the countertop. He shook his head and turned to him. Leaning against the counter, he took off his mitten and sighed. "Yes, I am happy, Anatoly." He ran his hand over his head and remembered his hair. "I'll be even happier when this grows back."

"It fits you," Anatoly smirked.

"What's going on with you? What have you been doing?" Dmitry pried.

The other cooks moved about in the kitchen around them fixing the other meals that would feed nearly one hundred people very soon. They knew to be silent, to be invisible around the men, although they listened on carefully to gossip about it later.

"I thought that maybe after the meeting and the news you might decide to come back is all...you know, come back for good," Anatoly coughed and looked around.

"Give us a minute, people," Dmitry ordered, realizing his son's discomfort. It had been a long time since he had to hide anything, now that he was living on the up and up.

The staff left the kitchen quietly.

Dmitry took the pickled cucumbers from the jar and placed them on the platters while he waited for his son to come clean. He turned his back to him, giving him time to get his thoughts straight.

"Why won't you come back, papa?" Anatoly pushed.

"I did. Just for you, but only for this deal."

"There is so much money to be made, so much power to be had. How can you just walk away?"

Dmitry grinned. "For a young man, I imagine that this seems to be priority but not for me – not anymore. I am filthy rich. And I am still extremely powerful." He turned to face his son. "And yet I need more than that. Like I told you, I am happy being here with family, raising my daughter, growing old with my wife, doing things that I never could do as boss. Even doing this favor is a lot to ask of me, even from my son, but I do it, because I love you and for no other reason than that."

"I don't know if I can do it without you." His statement was sincere. He clenched his jaw and looked down at the granite floor.

Dmitry's heart warmed. "You can do it. I would not have left you in charge if I felt you unworthy."

"I just…I don't understand how one woman can make a man want to leave his entire life behind or alter it in such a way. It's been three years, and I still don't understand."

Dmitry shook his head. His dimples deepened as he gave a hearty laugh. "You're just a kid, Anatoly. Give it time. When you meet the woman who completes you, you'll know it."

"How? I need to know this, so I can stay away from her always."

Dmitry walked beside his son and took the spoon from him. He took a deep breath and shook his head cleverly. "It will happen when you least expect, with whom you least expect and it will be…jolting. It will feel like heart attack.

She will mesmerize you, capture you in such a way, you could not harm her if you tried."

Anatoly looked up at his father curiously.

But his father continued with a grin on his face. "And you will smell like her when you come from three hours of being in city with her. And your father…he will know that you've been with her, because he smelled her cologne when she was trying to screw him the night before."

"I'm not in love with her," Anatoly argued. "That is not who I was talking about, papa."

"You know. I wasn't boss… I didn't build all of this, because I paid no attention to detail. It is the detail that determines whether or not you stay alive," he dropped a pinch of pepper into his borsht. "Don't tell, Royal. She'll kill you both, and I don't mean it figuratively. You had better keep her far from here and under lock and key."

"And you? Are you disappointed in me?"

"I think it is big mistake. She's dangerous, stupid and occasionally does coke. I can't see the beauty in a woman like that."

"I've done coke before."

"Well, no one ever accused you of being smart either, *junior*."

"Where you attracted to her?"

"Yes. I thought that she was very persuasive. If I had not been married to Royal, I would have had her."

"So, I am making mistake?"

"Colossal, but it is your call. I think if Royal had come on to you instead of me, you would have tried. That doesn't make you a bad man; it just makes you a man."

"I went to kill Victoria. For what she had done to Royal and the disrespect she had shown this family, I went to drug her and throw her in the woods somewhere or something."

"And you ended up doing what…what you did to Brigitte?"

"No," he shook his head in disgust. "No, I drugged and kidnapped her."

Dmitry frowned. "I told you that you didn't know a damned thing about women."

"I have to keep her there until I take her back to Memphis with me," he sighed and looked at his father, who was obviously flabbergasted by his idiotic move. "I sound so fucking stupid."

"It won't work, Anatoly. You should just let her go now. She is trouble, but the two of you together is a disaster."

"Who says I want it to work? I'm going to make her facilitate the buy of the art to clean the money. That's all."

"We don't allow women into the inner workings of the brotherhood. Not even Royal. It's almost sacrilegious. The men won't like it if you let her do anything more than you're saying.

You'll end up getting her killed and yourself. The code is the code."

"I'm only using her to cover my ass. I'll get rid of her in a few months."

"Bullshit."

"I don't love her."

"Can't help who you love."

"If I start to fall for her, I'll put bullet in her head."

Dmitry didn't say another word. He gave his son a disapproving look and tasted his borscht.

***

Royal washed her daughter's hair carefully, separating the delicate strands and brushing through the curly black locks one section at a time. She had been doting over Anya for over an hour now in the bathroom.

While the act was so small, it was so meaningful. Where had all the time gone? What had she been doing for months on end that she would have missed her small angel grow so much? The questions brought tears to her eyes. This was what she lived for, to be with the child that she nearly died for and would die for again over and over if she had to.

"Momma, why are being so nice?" Anya asked, squeezing her rubber ducky until it squealed and shot out water. "You are being my best friend again."

Royal smiled while inside her heart broke. "I'm sorry, Anya, for everything. I'm being nice, because I realize that I need to treat you more special than I have in the past."

"So you love me now?"

"I've always loved you." She turned her daughter's face towards her own and rubbed the water from her rosy cheeks. "Don't you know that Momma would do anything for you?"

"Yes," she said proudly. "And I'll do anything for you and Daddy. I'll be four next month. I can buy you both two white ponies."

"Just what we've always wanted," Royal brushed through her hair again. "It's quite a big feat to make it to four years old. We should have a big princess party for you."

"Did you have a princess party when you turned four?"

"No, I wasn't as special as you are."

"Momma, you are too special. Daddy says so all the time."

Dmitry walked into the bathroom and smiled at the sight of his wife and daughter. Grabbing a chair from across the room, he sat beside the tub and put a towel in his lap. "Let Papa dry you off, princess."

Royal helped her out of the large bathtub and into her father's arms, where he quickly covered her with the oversized towel. She wrapped her arms around his neck and kissed him.

"Love you, Daddy," she said, rubbing her nose on his.

"Oh, I love you too, my sweet one," he said, holding her tight. He looked up at his wife and saw hurt on her face.

"What's wrong?"

"Nothing. I just," she sighed. "I realize how much I've neglected my own daughter."

Dmitry dried Anya off and pulled her hair out of her face. "When I was child, I would have killed for the attention that you call neglect," he said cleverly. "And if you were to ask me, Anya doesn't look like she's going without much." He ran his large fingers over the carat diamonds in his daughter's ears.

Royal knew that he was just trying to make her feel better. She took her daughter out of his arms and put her on her hip. "I'm going to get her dressed, and we're going to go downstairs and have a great time. Aren't we, Anya." She smiled at him more warmly than she had in many years.

"Papa is making borscht for you," Dmitry added. "It's going to be great time."

"Do you know how lucky we are to have your father," Royal asked her daughter.

"Yep," Anya said cheerfully. "Daddy, you need to get dressed too. You can't wear that."

"I will honey, after Momma gets you dressed, she'll come back and help me with a few things," he explained. His eyes sparkled. "Then Daddy will help her get dressed and then we go down for party."

***

While every arrangement could be made down-stairs, and Anya helped the maids set the tables with beautiful Khokloma dishes, Royal and Dmitry were getting reacquainted with each other in the confines of their bedroom.

He stood across the dimly lit room by the bed undressing her with his eyes. His sensual looks made her blush, made heat rise from her body and singe her cheeks.

He had a way of clenching his wide jaw and staring at her that made her feel naked, even when she was fully dressed. He licked his lips and smirked. Naughty thoughts filled his head, making him dizzy with lust.

"I could get used to this," he confessed.

"So could I," she said, happy with herself.

"Are you…back for good, or is this a glimpse of what I could have had?"

She walked very slowly across the room, making him watch the sway of her hips and stood at his feet. Laying her hand on his lower chest, she watched him take a deep breath, like he was anticipating lightning and thunder.

"I'm back for good," she whispered. "Or at least for as long as you'll have me."

He grabbed her quickly and pulled her up in his arms. With a passionate sigh, he kissed her open mouth and laid her on the bed.

"Oh, I'll have you," he answered. "Every day for the rest of my life."

"It's strange. I don't know what happened. The thought of losing you to another woman made me realize how much I needed you. I've been so foolish, Dmitry. All I've thought about is myself and what I've gone through, but I didn't stop long enough to think about you and all that you've given up to be with me and Anya."

"I've given up nothing."

The words stung inside. He knew that they were true and that he was deceiving her even as he made love to her. The treachery was nauseating. Still, he hid his heavy burden in hopes that after the deal his secret would simply go away.

"You should never be ashamed of your sadness." He cringed. "The fact that you showed honest emotion and were not afraid to grieve for your many losses shows how much of a real woman you are. I could not have handled the same torture that you endured with such dignity."

Royal smiled. "Do you know in all the time that we've been together you have never said one mean thing to me? It's almost unreal. I mean, I know how much of a bitch that I've been. Don't think that I don't." They both laughed. "But you always are careful with me, never cruel."

"Why would I? You are the only woman who has ever sacrificed everything for me. And at such a high cost…"

"Let's not talk about that. Let's do what your eyes were saying a minute ago," she said, running her hands down to his jeans.

"I'm afraid what they were saying involved actions so distasteful, so…" he breathed in as he felt her slim hand slip inside of his pants and grasp his throbbing penis. "So you like distasteful, eh?"

"I adore it," she purred.

Chapter 14

Dawn broke the horizon and slipped through the heavy curtains in Anatoly's room. He stared up at the ceiling watching the large fan whirl above him. His mind was on Victoria. If he closed his eyes, he saw her. When he breathed, he smelled her perfume. The thought of that wicked bitch incited a riot throughout his entire body. Damn her to hell. He had to have her, even if just once.

The night before, his father had eyed him the entire dinner. And for some ungodly reason, Brigitte clung to him in a very subtle but irritating way. While everyone else was eating, drinking and talking, she sat close, smiled at him and continued to try to make conversation.

He had to end things with her, make her go away. His life was getting far too complicated. Just then he heard his door open.

He sat up in bed and watched as Brigitte closed the door behind her and leaned against the door in her baby blue uniform.

"*Bon jour*," she whispered with a wanting look upon her fair beautiful features.

Anatoly did not speak. Though he could not deny his constant enchantment by her utter bewitching good looks, he knew he was no good for her. He tapped the bed beside him and ran his hands through his hair.

She walked up to the bed and sat beside him. Rubbing his scruffy beard, she leaned in to kiss him, but he quickly moved.

"*Net*. We need to talk," his voice was flat.

"So talk," she said, feeling her stomach turn.

"We can't do this anymore." He met her bright eyes.

"Why?"

"You are good girl. You need man who will be faithful and loving and…take care of you. I will not. I may tell you that I will, but I won't."

"I don't want your money."

"I'm not talking about money. I'm talking about you."

"Anatoly…"

"I am not my father," he interrupted. "Don't think that what he does for my stepmother will translate to me and you. I'm not that sincere."

"I know. I just thought…"

"It won't work. I don't want it to."

"Did I do something?" Tears formed in the corner of her eyes and her small mouth quivered.

He scratched his forehead and frowned. "No. It's not you at all." *It's her*, he thought to himself. "How is your mother? Is she better?" he asked, wanting to change the subject. His decision had been made. This would end now.

"No. Pretty soon I'll be all alone in this world." Tears ran down her face. Closing her eyes, she dropped her head. It felt as though the entire world had just stopped spinning.

"Well, you'll always have my parents," he stood up. "I've got to shower and head out of here. I really am sorry, Brigitte." He rubbed her shoulder. "I'm still here if you need any-thing...*financially*."

"I won't." She stood up, straightened her uni-form and left.

***

Brigitte left Anatoly's room with her head up, but as soon as she closed the large doors behind her, the tears broke through and trickled down her face.

Lips twisted into a painful frown, she ran down the dark corridor to the kitchen -the only place she knew was vacant at this hour. Her feet carried her swiftly. She could feel her stomach twisting into knots as though she would vomit. The rain of tears evident on her face, ruining her makeup, she fled down the stairwell and down the back pathway to the kitchen.

Barging through the doors, she leaned on the counter and let out of agonizing sob. Damn him to hell for hurting her.

Dmitry took his spoon out of the peanut butter and whipped his head around the door of the cupboard to see Brigitte bent over the table crying.

Wiping his mouth, he placed the jar back in the far corner of his stash of treats and closed the door. Immediately, she stood up, out of breath and flushed.

In his robe, he walked over to her and sat down on a stool by the island. It didn't take a rocket scientist to know that either her mother had died, or Anatoly had struck. Based upon the mere rage in her eyes, he knew that it had something to do with the latter.

"Brigitte, what is the matter?" he asked in a tranquil, soothing voice.

She wiped her face quickly, embarrassed by her display of horrid, raw emotion. "Excuse me, sir, for my outburst. I thought I was alone," she explained between sniffs.

"You are not," he said, reached over to the large bowl to take out a few cherries. "Would you like one?"

"No," she said, blinking fast to stop the tears. "I'm sorry, sir."

"It's alright. I have wife and daughter. I see tears more than any other man in the world, besides maybe a pediatrician."

She laughed.

"So, what is wrong?   Has your mother passed?"

"No." She sighed. "Thank God. She still fights every single day." Forced to smile at her mother's strength, she finally stood up straight and smoothed out her wrinkled uniform.

"Then what would make your cry so badly at dawn?"

"Your son." She closed her eyes and clenched her jaw. "I'm afraid that I am just not good enough for him or bad enough."

Dmitry smiled. His beautiful features were laced with old wisdom. He popped the cherry seed out of his mouth into his hand and grabbed a napkin. "Did he tell you that, or did you assume it?"

"How can I assume anything different?   He broke up with me," she lamented.

"Brigitte, you are good girl. I assume he did it, because he cares for you, and he is not yet ready for responsibility of caring for such a good woman."

"You Medlov men use the term 'good girl' a lot." She nodded at him then looked up at the ceiling as she bit her lip. "But you offer no explanation as to why good is bad for you."

Dmitry raised his brow. "I think you know. Everyone who works for us knows. We are not men of respectable character. It is a curse to have a good woman at your side and find her hurt because of your misdeeds. The safest thing is to not allow her to be at your side."

"I've heard the stories. I do not care," she began to cry. "I would do anything to be with him."

"Why?"

"Because I love him."

"Why?"

"I don't know. I just do. And I was hoping that someday he would love me back."

"And because he knows that *that someday* will never come, he would no longer lead you on." He pushed the bowl down to her and watched her pull out a few cherries for herself. "This is sad that you have found yourself in love with someone who does not love you, but it is good also."

"How?" She wiped the tears from her mouth.

"Because you leave yourself open to find someone who does love you and will stand by you. Do not look at it as a negative. It is simply God's way of leading you to right person."

"Of course, you can speak like this when you have a woman like Mistress Medlov to love. She is strong and beautiful, and she loves you more than even herself." Brigitte feared she had said too much but could not stop.

"Your words are kind. To know that you have known this since before our reconciliation makes me...happy. But do you see how pained she has been for years?"

"Yes."

"It is because of me. And Anatoly will not see you pained in same way. For that, I am proud of him and happy for you. Trust me, your feelings for him will dull in months if not weeks. After all, he has never properly presented you in public. Every woman deserves to be presented, whether the man is poor or rich has nothing to do with his pride in his selection. When you find man who treats you like queen, regardless of his status in world, you have found the man you should spend rest of your life with...not a man who will have you in is bed but not in his life."

Dmitry's words were sobering and broken. His English was always worse when he first woke up, when no one was around to correct him, namely Royal. But his words caused her to sit up straighter and feel better about herself.

She nodded at him with a brighter smile in her cloudy eyes.

"Thank you, Master Medlov."

"It is my pleasure," he said, standing up. "Now, if you'll excuse me."

He had been around enough young vulnerable women for the week. He had no intention of being accused being with Anatoly's maid.

"Yes, sir," she said as he walked pass. She watched him as he left, moving with ease through the world, comfortable in his own skin, knowledgeable, wise and beautiful. It made her ask herself why she couldn't have a man like him. Then she thought of Royal and how absolutely irrefutable she was in everyway. *Maybe that's why*, she said to herself.

***

Anatoly parked his car in the garage and grabbed the grocery bags out of the trunk. He headed up the stairs and entered into the condo to smells of food burning on the stove. After turning off the alarm, he set the bags down on the kitchen table and turned off the asparagus burning in the skillet.

"Oh, shit. I was coming to get that," Victoria said, rounding the corner. She looked up at him and smiled as she walked pass.

Again, he caught a whiff her intoxicating cologne. He eyed her as she went over and looked into the cloth bags to pull out the produce.

"I figured you might be hungry," he explained, pointing at the bags.

"I am. Thanks," she said, sorting through the food.

"Did you call anyone, email anyone?"

"No."

"I don't suppose that you would tell me if you did."

She sighed and leaned against the kitchen table. "No, I don't think that I would."

Anatoly looked down and smirked. "I see that you're still a smart ass."

"Sorry." She swallowed hard, remembering the gun shots from the night before. "You have that effect on me. I don't know. You make me crazy."

He smiled. "I have the feeling that you were crazy well before you met me."

"You might be right."

Anatoly remembered himself.

"I didn't come here to make unneeded conversation with you." His jaw clenched. "I told you that you'd be working for me, and I need to give you instructions for your first assignment."

"You make it sound like mission impossible."

Victoria walked over and poured herself a cup of coffee.

Anatoly noticed that she was wearing one of his dress shirts and a pair of his boxers. He could see the definition in her muscular legs and her perfectly smooth dark skin better now. Looking up at her face, he tried to focus on his thoughts.

"Want some coffee?" her eyelashes fluttered like butterfly wings.

"I don't drink coffee." He looked away again.

"*Oooookay*." She went back over to the kitchen table and sat down. "Do I need a pen and pad or something?"

"Never write down anything that I don't tell you to. You have to learn how to remember."

Victoria sighed. "Alright." She took a sip of her coffee and eyed him.

Anatoly didn't walk over to her. He preferred the space.

"You are going to fly to Sochi, Russia tomorrow night to purchase one piece of very important, very expensive art under an assumed name with a designated account. You following me?"

"Yeah, that's where the Olympics are taking place right?"

"Yes, but you won't be there for that. You're going to an art show, and then you're going to fly back here."

"Okay. What is this important piece of art?"

"It's by an up and coming artist from Moscow named Phitznas. The piece is a large gold-plated bust with emeralds, diamonds...all sorts of precious stones. There will be several bidders, but your bid will be the highest."

"How much?"

"$550 million."

Victoria choked on her coffee and looked up. While she wasn't familiar with the art world, the thought of spending that much money on one piece blew her mind.

Anatoly rolled his eyes. "Just make the bid under the name that I give you. Our broker will accompany you. You won't have any problems with the transaction. They will take you to the back of the studio to finish the purchase. After that, you will get in the car and be immediately escorted out of the country."

"Is that it?"

"For now. Now, get dressed. I need to go over with you how to make bid, pay and what all is expected of you, and I can't do that with you nearly naked."

Victoria looked down at her lack of clothes and smiled.

Chapter 15

Dmitry, Royal and Anya piled into the family Land Rover and headed into the city for a day of work. It had been months since they had done so, and while the task was simple enough, it brought all of them great joy. They were a family again with things to do and places to go.

Royal sat in the passenger seat going through her to-do list while Dmitry listened to talk radio and drove. Anya watched a movie on the small screen attached to her mother's chair and brushed her doll's hair.

"Will you have lunch with me today?" Dmitry asked.

"Of course," Royal looked up at him with a bright glow on her face. "Anya and I will come over at about noon."

"Good," he rubbed his blonde beard. His mind was wrapped around his secret, boiling inside of him like a guilty stew. He looked over at her, unsuspecting and trusting again and felt a twinge in his stomach. There was nothing worse than deceit.

"Baby, I..." his voice dragged.

"Daddy, will you fix me the bow tie pasta for lunch like on the commercial?" Anya asked, interrupting Dmitry.

"That's Italian food, sweetheart," he said, losing his nerve.

"Well, will you fix it?" her voice was high and eager.

"Yes. I'll send out for it this morning."

"Thanks, Daddy."

Royal looked over at him and put down her notepad. "Is something wrong?" She could see the frown he was trying desperately to hide.

He glanced over at her for a moment and took a deep breath. "No," he said, scooting over in his seat farther away. "Everything is fine. Why do you ask?"

"You have that look on your face."

"What look?"

"Like...I don't know...something's wrong."

Dmitry paused. He could tell her now and watch Royal's new found glow diminish back into a jaded darkness. He could watch her build the wall again – so tall and so thick that he would never be able to break it down, or he could just finish this last deal and move on with their lives.

He smiled wide and bright, his dimples deepened and his bright blue eyes sparkled. "Things couldn't be better, really."

"Sure?"

"*Da.*"

"Okay. I must be losing my women's intuition." Royal smiled and picked her notepad back up.

I must be crazy, Dmitry thought to himself as he focused on the road.

***

News from Prague indicated that Anatoly had arrived on yesterday and the Medlov Chateau was located right outside the city. As soon as Dorian received the information, he packed a bag and hopped a private jet to the Czech. He couldn't trust anyone else to do this type of reconnaissance for him. He needed to get up close and personal-see how the enemy lived for himself.

Dorian stared at himself in the mirror of the hotel bathroom, stared at his face, his eyes, his mouth – all slightly aged with time. He wondered who he had become in three years, because he was not at all the man he used to be. He was successful, powerful, rich and still he was empty.

The treacherous murder of Royal Stone had haunted him like a ghost, reminded him that he would burn in hell for his dealings with Ivan and his desire to turn a blind eye and a deaf ear to what he knew his long-time friend would do and did do that fateful night.

If he could have, Dorian would have simply avoided Dmitry for the rest of his life. He would have been more than pleased never to mingle or do business in any circle that the *Russian* dwelled, but it had gone too far. He had to finish this now.

His plan was simple. He would spend exactly one day in Prague meeting with the man who would place the bomb on Dmitry's plane before he left the city, then fly back to Sochi to prepare for the transaction tomorrow.

His liaison would facilitate the buy and once the funds had been confirmed, the Medlov's would request an audience with the go-between, which was him. When he revealed himself, Dmitry would be incensed, but the deal would already have gone through and his clients would be out of the loop.

He would then tell Anatoly where to have his people pick up the shipment and then Dmitry would wage war. Only the *Russian* will be out-gunned, out manned and outsmarted. He will leave Sochi immediately and head back to Prague. Then his private jet will explode and go down in smoke over the Black Sea.

Nothing will be provable except that they had a rivalry. Anatoly will be forced to move on, Dmitry will be dead, and he can finally move on with his own life or what was left of it. There will surely be remnants of an after taste to deal with, even the possibility of the murder of Anatoly. But the biggest threat will be out of the way and either way, the family will fall.

***

After dropping Royal and Anya off, Dmitry headed into his restaurant and immediately began to cook. His staffed danced about him as he prepared for a long day and a hot date with the two ladies of his life. While his hands stayed busy, his mind wrapped around him like a thick fog. His son was about to rise to the highest level achievable in organized crime, and he was about to help him.

A few years ago, before the birth of Anya, it would have been his proudest moment. Now, he fought within himself over what he was making - a monster of a massive proportions. He would never allow his daughter to break the law even once, and yet he was preparing his son to be the epitome of criminal.

The irony was more than a notion. If he made his son back out, it could cost many people their lives. If he pushed him forward and made sure the deal was completed, it could cost many people their lives. If he did nothing, he could lose his son. If he did anything, he could lose.

It would have helped to have Royal to talk to about the matter, since had become his closest confidant and dearest friend. And even though she didn't know it, she was very sound in most of her decisions. She was his rock, and yet he deceived her. His actions made him question his very sanity or at the very least his loyalty.

***

Anya played in the mirror, dressed in a pair of her mother's heels, while Royal stood in the dressing room with a duchess and her assistant picking out gowns for an upcoming event. It felt extraordinary to Royal to be back in her favorite place doing what she felt she did best-running her own business. The staff had been surprised to see her but ecstatic for her return.

She immediately started to reorganize the shop, making lists and ordering new products. The day had all but whizzed past her when she looked down are realized that it was half past eleven.

After getting the duchess's order and seeing her out, Royal prepared to go and have lunch with Dmitry. Just as she was about to grab her coat, a tall black man entered into to the shop.

Everyone stopped when the door closed behind him. Royal looked up stunned. It was not as if a black man had never shopped at Royal Flush. It wasn't that he was black at all. It was simply that he was beautiful.

Beautiful people bothered Royal. Ivan was beautiful and *rotten*. Dmitry was beautiful and *dangerous*. Anatoly was beautiful and *cold*.

Now, a strange man entered her shops with his eyes planted on her, and the only word that could possibly describe him was beautiful. But there had to be something else. *Beautiful and crazy. Beautiful and gay. Beautiful and what?* She could go on but stopped herself. The amusement in her quest was most inappropriate for the time.

The man seemed startled by Royal. It was as if he knew her. She looked over at Anya first, always thinking of her little one. In a quick motion, she snapped her slender, long fingers together and pointed at the back. Obediently, her daughter dashed to the back office without asking one question.

"May I help you?" she finally asked with less than a welcoming smile on her face.

Dorian was lost for words. Her face had been burned into his memory. It was impossible to forget her or her untimely death. It had been the thing that had haunted him for three long years.

It was just dumb luck that once he arrived in Prague he had been told that Dmitry owned not only a restaurant but also a dress shop. He had planned on just stopping in to see some homage paid to a dead girlfriend; instead he had found a living, breathing replica of the woman who had scarred them all.

"Sir?" Royal asked with her hands folded in front of her.

The diamond necklace that Dmitry that bought her years ago to hide the scars Ivan had given her blinded Dorian as he walked closer.

"This is Royal Flush?" he asked in a deep rich Russian baritone that captivated the other women in the shop but worried Royal.

"This is." She stopped in her tracks. "How may we help you?"

Dorian tried hard not to blatantly stare at the striking woman, but he could not help himself. She appeared older, more seasoned, more knowledgeable than the pictures from many years ago. It was her eyes. They were dark and sinister now, no doubt because of Ivan.

"I want to buy a dress for my fiancée," explained. His voice was like silk in an odd baritone.

Ivan had told Dorian about his first experience with Royal many years ago at her previous shop in Memphis, how he had rudely made sexual advances towards her. It was because of this that Dorian was very careful and respectful with his tone though he wanted to ask her a million questions.

"Is it for a particular event?" Royal asked with a sinister look in her eyes. She didn't trust him at all.

"A night on the town. We've just arrived here in Prague for the weekend, and I'd like to surprise her," he said, taking his eyes off her and looking around the boutique. "I was hoping for something elegant, black *of course*, but not gaudy. I like classic beauty, you know...the timeless type." He thought the description fit Royal perfectly.

"Well, I'm sure that we can accommodate you with that," Royal said, turning to her assistants. "Ladies, let's pull a few collections in black." She turned back to the stranger. "What size?"

He smiled cleverly. "She's in between a six and an eight."

Royal nodded. "Six and eight, ladies."

The women scurried around and left the two to talk. Royal gave him a curious and untrusting half smirk as she went behind the counter. Inside, she was screaming for space. He was so familiar to her, yet she was sure that she had never laid eyes on him.

"So where are you from?" She tried to calm her anxiety.

"Moscow," he answered, walking over to the counter. "And yourself?"

"So many places," she pulled out a few collections of jewelry and began strategically placing them on the counter for him to shop thorough.

"You'll want a nice necklace, pair of earrings or some jewelry to accompany your dress," she said without looking up at him. "We can provide you everything you need and have it delivered to your hotel this evening before seven."

His eyes burned through her. "You sound American," his voice was low. "*Southern American.*"

She looked up at him. "I would suggest platinum jewelry. It's popular this season." Her eye twitched.

Dorian bit his lip. "Pick something. I'll buy it."

"Do you have a budget?"

"No. I'm not the budget type."

Royal grabbed the most expensive set of earrings, a necklace and bracelet in the case and placed them in a box. She could feel him staring at her. She finally looked up and sighed. "Memphis," she confessed. The truth longed to break free. She felt vindicated by saying it. "I'm from Memphis, Tennessee." She stood up a little straighter.

"Home of the blues," he smiled. "It's hot as hell there."

"So you've been?"

"Yes," he nearly whispered. "A few years back." He eyed her.

"How many *years* back?"

"Almost three and a half now."

Royal cleared her throat and moved the long strands of hair falling out of her bun. "I was long gone by then." She pushed the box across the counter. "This set is very charming. She'll be pleased at your selection."

Dorian reached into his jean pocket and pulled out his wallet. He put down a black American Express card on the counter and pushed it over to her fingertips.

Royal did not speak for a minute. So many thoughts passed through her head and her heart beat at such a painfully fast pace until words would have been far too much of a struggle.

He breathed as hard as she did. His thoughts were unreadable but desperate. With his hand still on the card, he eyed her as she looked down, refusing to make eye contact.

"I'm at the Hotel Iron Gate in the Royal Suite," his thoughts lingered on after his words, but he forced himself to stop talking, afraid to say too much or the wrong thing.

"We'll have it delivered tonight," she said, finally looking up as she took his card.

"Is that your beautiful daughter you sent to the back?"

"Yes," Royal said, even more worried now.

"She looks *well*." His jaw clenched.

"She is. Thank you."

Royal watched the women come out of the back with an assortment of black dresses and walk to the sitting room where he could pick through them. He looked away from her for a moment and then looked back. He wanted to say something, but what he could he say?

"My assistants are very capable. I'll leave them to help you." She walked from behind the counter and headed towards the back. "Thank you for your business."

Dorian didn't speak. He watched her until she disappeared in the back and then calmly walked over to the sitting room to pick out a dress for his fictitious fiancée.

Chapter 16

The restaurant was only a block over from the boutique. Bundled up tightly, Royal carried Anya to see her father for their lunch date. The wind beat against them as they huddled together under large furs and rushed through the cobblestone lane to the warm welcoming Russian restaurant on the corner.

As soon as they entered, the hostesses took their coats and greeted them. Then they were escorted back to their normal table, where Dmitry had placed a large bouquet of roses for his lovely pair.

When they were seated, Dmitry came out of the kitchen with one staff member and several trays of food. One special plate had bowtie pasta and alfredo sauce for Anya.

"Hello, Mrs. And Ms. Medlov," Dmitry greeted with a bright smile. "How was your morning?"

Royal hesitated. Something about the strange man made her feel as though she should instantly tell Dmitry, but something else told her to hold her secret.

"We had a very interesting day," she finally answered.

"I wore big shoes, daddy," Anya explained. "And they had diamonds on them."

"Diamonds?"

"Big, big diamonds."

Royal smiled but was quiet.

"I know your momma sells some expensive digs over there, but I didn't know that she sold diamond shoes," Dmitry bent over and kissed Royal on the forehead.

She ran her hand through her daughter's long black locks of silky hair. "It's part of the new Anya Only Collection," Royal said, trying to play the part and rid herself of the memories of the stranger.

Dmitry noticed a sort of disconnected daze on Royal's face but chose not to comment further. He was sure, when it was time, she would tell him. Instead, he served them a wonderful meal and sat down to have lunch with his family.

                              ***

Dorian left the boutique soon after his meeting with Royal and quickly jumped on his motorcycle to head across town to the airport's private airstrip. His heart was in the bottom of his chest after seeing that his ghost was not only still alive but also had given birth to Dmitry's daughter, a child that he swore belonged solely to Ivan. It made him wonder if the girl was his old friend's.

He admonished himself and tried to focus. His planned could nearly be ruined if he allowed himself to unravel. But the woman was strikingly beautiful, so much so that he instinctively wanted her for himself. Thou shalt not covet. He heard the words in his head as he drove through the streets of Prague.

Had he forgotten himself so much that he could not remember his commandments? He held himself to a higher standard than most, hence his nickname as a holy man, yet he found himself wanting Dmitry's wife so badly until he could taste her perfume in the back of his throat.

He was certain that she did not know who he was, but what if she went back and told Dmitry about him coming into the boutique? Something in her eyes promised that she would not.

For now, he had to stick to his plan. He had a meeting with an aircraft pilot in forty minutes. The deal was that the man would receive a small fortune for simply not showing up for work on tomorrow morning, leaving his clothes and passes for another person to use.

The bomb would be placed on Dmitry's jet and detonated after it left Sochi. The plan was flawless, all accept for the possibility of Royal being on it, or even Dmitry's daughter. The possibility of a second chance from God to redeem himself from his horrid sins seemed to be clouded by revenge. He needed to pray, to figure out why things had happened as they had.

***

When Dorian was finished at the airport, he gave his assistant a call to follow through with things as planned. She did so swiftly. Within the hour, she had notified Anatoly about the meeting set for tomorrow night in Sochi.

Anatoly was ready. He nodded at Victoria and put down his cell phone. She sat across from him in living room on the couch wearing one of Royal's cashmere dresses. He cleared his throat and picked another cigarette up to light it.

"That was phone call we were waiting for," Anatoly confirmed. "You flight out tomorrow. I'll arrange for a first class ticket for you. Don't be late. Don't fuck up."

Victoria raised her brow. "I won't." She watched him pour another shot of vodka as he smoked his cigarettes. His blue eyes squinted as inhaled the nicotine. "What's next? After this, what I am supposed to do?"

"You go to Memphis with me. I told you." His voice was a growl.

Victoria rolled her eyes and grabbed the back of her neck to massage her aching muscles. Her dark, thick hair fell over on her arm, catching Anatoly's eye.

He looked over at her and put down his glass. There was an inquisitive look on his chiseled face. He clenched his jaw and tilted his head, puzzled by the woman.

"What?"she asked, realizing he was eyeing her.

"Why are you the way that you are?"

Victoria frowned. "What *way* am I?"

Anatoly took another drag from his cigarette. "Twisted. Damaged."

She bit her lip. "I don't know. Why are you the way that you are?"

"I think it's genetic. It could be inferiority complex. Mostly, it's just because I like money."

"So you admit that you're fucked up?"

"Yeah," he said quickly.

"And you like woman who are?"

Anatoly nodded. "I *think* I do." He was sincere. "I feel like most good women are too good for me and most of the others are out to get something."

"Well, at least you're honest," she said, scratching her head. She sat up straight and crossed her legs as he waited for his answer. They were silent for a moment. He watched her go through the motions before she finally spoke.

"My father never gave me the attention that I wanted. My mother never thought that anything I did was good enough," she smirked. "I know it sounds beyond elementary, but being twisted, as you call it, was a release for me. I mean, I went to top schools, got great grades, had a fucking five year plan from hell," she laughed and sighed. "But it just wasn't good enough."

"According to them?" he asked.

"Yeah, I originally started to travel abroad and take care of kids to get away, but then I saw that there was a hell of a lot of money involved in men who had fallen for the help and wanted to make it all go away after they had played for awhile and gotten bored."

"My father's no saint, but he would never cheat on his wife."

"I know," she laughed. "Boy, do I know." She cringed. "They're a really weird couple."

"Tell me about it," he said, shaking his head. "So, you got back at papa by sleeping with his friends and bleeding them dry."

"Basically."

"Hey, it is five year plan too," he said, offering her a glass of vodka.

"Like you said, I'm *twisted*."

She stood up and walked across the room to him to take the glass. He clenched it in his hand and looked up at her.

"What do you do about real relationships if you're always making them up?"

"I don't believe in real relationships." She looked him in his eyes. "They don't last."

"Sounds like your heart's been broken."

"Crushed." She took the glass. "I take it your heart hasn't."

"No. Never had that problem."

"Well good for you." She gulped down the vodka and looked away with her hands on her hips. "I'm sure that just because your heart hasn't been broken, it doesn't mean that you haven't broken a few."

Anatoly thought about Brigitte - the last name on his long list of victims.

"What was his name?" Anatoly asked, still looking up at her. He preferred for the conversation to never focus on him. It kept him from feeling guilty or feeling anything.

"It isn't important." She turned and looked at him. "Do you mind if I pack some of your stepmother's things for tomorrow. You never did let me go back to my hotel to pick up my own stuff."

"I forgot about that. I'll send for them, but for now, *Da*, just pack whatever is in there."

"It's not like my stuff is better than hers, really. It's like a freaking runway fashion show in her closet," Victoria explained. She turned to walk away and stopped at the doorway. Anatoly was still sitting, brooding over something quietly.

"Do you mind if I have one more drink?"

"No," Anatoly pulled the corked top off the vodka and reached out for her glass.

She walked back over directly in front of him and gave him her glass. She was much closer this time. He felt her skin against his.

Anatoly poured the vodka. The sound of the potent contents ran smoothly into the shot glass in the silence of the room. He set the bottle down then sat back in the chair. She was still standing in front of him, in between his open legs. He controlled his breathing, but he could feel the familiar heat rising at his collar.

She finished the shot and set it down on the table beside them. Then, slowly, she leaned in. He watched her closely as she snaked into him.

"What's one night, right?" she said, moving into his body to kiss him.

Anatoly felt her body lean against his. The contact made him grunt a little. Her slim long temple was warm to the touch.

"Don't..."Anatoly finally objected, turning his neck away from her soft lips. He could feel her breath on his skin.

"Why? It doesn't mean anything." She inhaled his cologne and kissed his cheek.

"That's exactly why," he explained. His minty breath tickled her nose.

She looked at him in his memorizing blue eyes. They were face-to-face now, and she could see that behind the tough exterior there was a young man who actually wanted to be loved.

She bit her lip and sighed. "People lie, you know." She hoped he read her thoughts. I do care, she whispered in her mind, but she would never say so aloud.

"All the time," he whispered.

She could feel his hot breath on her skin but he did not move towards her. Finally, she planted her hand against the chair to push herself up, embarrassed at her feeble attempt to persuade him. Refused by both father and son – what a loser, she thought.

His strong hand grasped her waist. Anatoly looked up at her and pulled her back down on his body. He slipped his free hand behind her head and pulled her mouth to his lips.

The hunger in his kiss startled her. It wasn't slow and sweet like Dmitry's. It was full of fire and vigor, bruising her lips, sucking her tongue, tasting the inside of her fleshy orifice.

His grip was powerful and found its way to her hair, pulling her body further down into his lap, onto his erection. She melted.

His kiss moved from her lips, to her chin, to her neck. His hot tongue brushed against her soft brown skin as his hands pulled her dress up just above her buttocks.

Their breathing escalated. His hand massaged her round buttocks and felt the smooth wetness in between her thighs. He could not stop. With a yank of her panties, he tore them off and slipped his fingers into her body. She closed her eyes and moaned, only to feel him pull the dress off of her.

Breasts exposed, she planted her knees on either side of him in the chair as he tasted the brown tips of her nipples. She moaned and arched her back. He bit her, nibbled at her skin. The pain radiated from her breasts to the tips of her toes.

She ran her hands through his curly, dark hair and then lifted his face to kiss him again. Her hands unbuttoned his shirt and revealed his muscular tan chest donning a plethora of tattoos. Sexy. So very sexy.

Anatoly picked her and himself up in one motion and laid her on the floor. He couldn't bring himself to wait long enough to carry her to the bedroom. He had to have her now.

She watched him as his trousers fell to the floor revealing tanned muscular legs. He fished out a condom, slid it on and kicked off his pants and underwear. He wasn't modest, didn't give a damn about the way things looked. He only wanted her.

Pushing her legs open, he leaned into her body and felt her naked flesh against his own for the first time. She was soft like silk. Unable to help himself, he ran his hands over her smooth bikini line. She kept herself up very well. If he knew her better, he would have tasted her mouthwatering brown mound, but he quickly decided against it.

Victoria arched her hips, awaiting his entry. What did she care that he was not into oral. There was only one thing on her mind. The ten inch phallic form standing upright before her. He came to her hastily, surging into her without words or theatrics. He filled her quickly, pulsating as he did. He dug his knees into the fine plush carpet and groaned.

Victoria let out a long whimper. He was exceedingly large. His muscular, vein-filled hips pushed into her body with hard pumps that rocked her and burned her back against the carpet with the rapid friction.

Fingers splayed out on his wide back, she held on as he ripped through her body. The ecstasy of his strong strokes made a sensual moan erupt from her throat.

He covered her mouth with a kiss and slipped a finger behind her into her buttocks. She looked up startled. *So, he was a kinky bastard.* She loved the foreign, naughty exhilaration but would deny him the pleasure he silently asked for. Not yet. Not tonight.

She finally pushed against his chest and made him roll over. Straddling him, she felt both his hands on her hips, pushing her down on top of him. He planted his feet and lifted them both off the floor. She pushed back, eager to ride him, moving her hips wildly on top of him.

Anatoly clenched his jaw and bucked back. He watched her body soar into the air in slow motion. With nearly the same force, she pushed back against his force again, making him fall to the ground.

He understood what she was doing – fighting for dominance. He wouldn't give it to her, unless she gave him what he wanted, and he had a feeling that she would not. So, he would make her suffer.

He quickly flipped her on her side and pulled her thick thighs back towards him. He could feel the tension in her body. She was afraid of how he would take her, but he would control his carnal desires – at least for tonight. Now beside her, he entered her warm vagina again and wrapped his arm around her small perky breasts.

The power made her clamor in his embrace. He pushed inside of her again and again until she felt a tremor from deep inside her body. She tried to pull away, but the agile young man pulled her to her knees and laid her on the couch where he took her from behind. One of his large hands was wrapped into a fist around her black hair and the other slapped against her brown, perfect buttocks, splattering the sweat that ran down from her back.

In perfect view of her long temple, he opened her wide, pulled back, and then felt her body began to vibrate. She clawed the sofa as she climaxed. The wetness of her body made for warmer more vivid sensations for him. He groaned as he watched, amazed at the contrast of their skin colors, the heat of her skin, the look of her.

Screaming his name as he picked her little body up, he pulled it into his rock hard erection. She was now not on the floor or the sofa but suspended in the air, trapped in his embrace. He held her close as he came. With his face against her back and his long arms cradling her, he caught his breath and moved her long hair out of his way.

When he was done, she sat in his lap, covered in sweat and drained. He picked her up off his penis sat her on the couch gently, exhibiting the last bit of strength that she had failed to deplete.

"Now you can go pack," he said, clearing his throat. His face was stone-like.

She looked across at him stunned and speechless.

***

"Lunch was great," Royal said, leaning into Dmitry as he bent to kiss her lips.

"*Da*? You liked? Good. We'll have leftovers tonight for dinner," he rubbed through her hair and looked in her eyes. She looked flushed.

"Are you getting sick?"

"A cold maybe. I feel...hot," she lied. "Listen. I'm so behind at the shop until I need to stay later. I'll get one of the girls to bring me home tonight. If Anya could stay with you for the rest of the day that would be great."

"Of course. Just make sure that you don't end up at the shop tonight alone. If I need to, I'll leave here and stay with you until you finish."

"No," she said quickly. "The girls will stay with me. You go home and take Anya. I'll be there shortly."

"Okay," Dmitry felt Anya tugging at his leg. "Yes, baby, what is it?" He looked down at her.

"Can I help Javier wash the dishes?" Anya asked, interrupting her parents.

"No," Royal answered, rubbing Anya's head. "Stay out of the way and be a good girl."

Dmitry smiled. "See you tonight."

Royal left the restaurant quickly and headed towards the boutique in an eager stride.

While she had every intention of going back to Royal Flush, it was only to get the clothes that the stranger had purchased and hand-deliver them to him. There were things that had not been said, that needed to be said. He knew more than he led on, and she intended to find out what.

***

Dorian stood in the shower letting the hot water drench his tired muscles and relieve the tension in his back. That damned woman was still on his mind, even after many hours of planning to kill her husband. Her heart-shaped lips, her chocolate skin, her full breasts. They were features drawn from a comic book, so pronounced and beautiful. Three years of Dmitry's constant doting had done her well.

She looked like she did not have a care in the world until you looked into her dark eyes. They spoke volumes. They spoke of Ivan. He knew that it was Royal the moment he laid eyes on her. She looked like the woman in the photos only less innocent now, much less innocent. But he wanted to immediately reach out and kiss her. It was a strange reaction, and he was ashamed of it, but he could not deny his utter attraction to Dmitry's muse. She made him think of what it would be like to have his own family. After all, he was forty now. No wife. No children.

Dmitry was a lucky man. If he had Royal, even for just one night...

The door bell rang. He wiped the water from his face and turned off the shower. Wrapping a towel around his waist, he grabbed his gun and walked slowly to the door.

He looked out the peep hole to find Royal standing on the other side of the door. He stood back. Was this a trap? Or was it something else? He opened the door just enough to see her face.

"Your dress, sir," Royal said, holding up the dress bag. "And your jewelry for the soon-to-be Mrs. Oriachiav."

"Of course," Dorian said, looking behind her. "Are you alone?"

"Yes," she sighed. "Open the door. I know there's no one in there." Her voice was firm and low.

He paused then opened it, standing out of the way for her to pass. She walked in with the bags and looked around the suite.

Laying the dress across the nearest table, she turned around and looked at him. "I came to talk," she said, taking a seat. "But I'm sure that you already know that. It's the only reason you told me where to find you."

Dorian stood soaking wet with only a damp towel covering his large body. He wasn't nearly as tall as Dmitry, but he was a devastatingly handsome, milk-chocolate, muscular man with wavy hair, full lips, brilliantly bright brown eyes and chiseled features that made him appear to be more of a model than a mafia figure.

He clenched his towel tightly forbidding it to show the evident bulge between his large thighs. She was no longer a modest woman. She gawked at him outright, assessing all of his assets, making mental note all of his features. She drank him in without looking away.

"*Goodness* woman, where are you manners?" he asked finally.

"I don't know what you mean," she lied. "If you feel uncomfortable, you should probably go and get dressed." She crossed her legs and gave him a snooty look.

"How do I know that I trust you to sit there and not snoop until I return, huh?"

"Fine. Dress here," she crossed her arms. "I've only seen two men naked in my adult life. I'd be obliged to see one who wasn't biologically related to a Medlov."

"And I thought that you should be afraid of me," he said sarcastically.

"Well..."

He smirked. At least she had a since of humor. He dropped his towel and walked to the duffle bag only steps away from her to retrieve his underwear. Her eyes bulged out of her head as she watched his well-endowed manhood flop lazily across this thigh. There was clear satisfaction on her face.

In her mind, she could not help but think of Dmitry kissing that whore of a woman, Victoria. Suddenly, she felt vindicated.

"This is inappropriate," he said, slipping on his boxers. "You should be ashamed."

"I'm not," she said, stoned faced. "I enjoyed that. *Spasiba*. Now, on to my questions. Why are you here? Who are you? Where do you know the Medlov's from? What are your intentions? Where's your fucking fiancée?"

"Slow down," he raised his hand. "Please." Running his hand over his head, he grabbed his cargo pants and slipped them on. "Now that I'm at least presentable, would you care for anything to drink?"

"No. This isn't a social visit. I want to know what the hell you know about me."

"Nothing."

"Don't lie to me. Tell me the truth," she breathed heavily. "Or I'll call *him*. I'll tell him that I'm here and when he gets here, I'll still

know who you are — right before he kills you.
You might as well do it the easy way."

"I'm a business partner." He clenched his jaw
and leaned over to her. "You need to be very,
very careful about what threats you make."

"Oh, I know about threats. And unfortu-
nately for you, they don't scare me anymore."
She swallowed hard. "Now, what's your real
name?"

"Dorian." He stood up.

"Why did you come to my shop?" she eyed
his hairy six-pack.

"When I got here, I heard that Dmitry had
another dress shop. It's was too coincidental. So
I came here to see for myself. I thought you were
dead many years ago." He went to his bag and
pulled out a t-shirt.

"I did die." Tears formed at the corners of her
eyes. "Ivan killed me."

"I know." They made eye contact. "What
Ivan did that day has haunted us all. At least, it
has haunted me. I must confess to you that I had
some idea of what he would do, but never did I
think that he would take it to that extent. Once
we all heard, it was too late. No one could
believe the carnage that he left behind. We were
all damned, and it was because we had done
nothing to save you."

"Save me?"

"An innocent. You should have been left out of the war, especially when we heard the news of your pregnancy."

"Who is *we*?"

"*We*...everyone in the community in which your husband lived. You must not realize the power that he had...has." He smirked.

"No. I, pretty much, live a bottle. So why does all this change now? Why are you hear, Dorian?"

He slipped on the shirt and grabbed a seat. "Has Dmitry returned? Is coming back to the Vory? I need to know." He sat in the chair backwards and leaned his body against it.

"I don't know. He seemed differently lately, but not *that* different. I thought that he was done with all of that."

"Understand, I would have been happy to stay away from him for the rest of my life, but his son made the best offer. My clients would not refuse. I know once Dmitry sees me, a war will begin again. And while I am no coward, I assure you that, I feel compelled to try to stop this before it starts. However, once it starts, he leaves me no choice."

Royal looked him in his chestnut colored eyes and listened as he told her about the deal, about his old dealings with Dmitry through Ivan, about the botched assassination attempts and about the bombs he placed inside of Dmitry's restaurant in Memphis to kill the entire Medlov crime family three years prior.

Royal was flabbergasted. She sat petrified, unable to speak.

"I don't why I am telling you all of this. I guess for me, I thought God would punish me because of what happened to you. But now I see you and you are alive and I feel compelled to fix this, only I'm not sure how," Dorian explained.

"I know how," Royal said finally in whisper. She looked up at him. "I'll get to Sochi tomorrow. If you agree to form a truce with my family and my son's *crime family*..." She shook her head in disgust and cringed. "Then I can persuade the two of them to let bygones be bygones, and we all walk away from this with no more to do with each other."

"I'm not sure such a truce would hold. Your outlook seems more optimistic than things really work."

"It's better to try than to knowingly allow bloodshed again, isn't it? Dmitry would never go back on his word, if he promised me or anyone. He's not that type of man."

"Didn't he promise you? He's gone back the Vor- for all we know, for good."

"It was to save Anatoly. I know it. I just do. He doesn't want that anymore. He wants us."

"Okay." He shook his head. "Okay. Yeah. If you are in Sochi with him tomorrow, and you can make them agree to a truce, then I'll do it. But it has to be after the deal is completed. Otherwise, my clients will kill us all. If you don't show, I'm sorry. I can only say that I tried."

"I understand." She stood up. "Thank you."

"For what?"

"For giving us a chance to live again. For not doing what Ivan did to us."

He smiled. "I have only one request. And I know it's selfish but..."

"Okay," she stepped closer to him.

"As a signal to let me know that you are still on my side, wear the dress that I bought."

She looked over at the dress bag. "It's awfully formal."

"So is the place that we're meeting. You'll fit in perfectly."

"And it's at that hotel you were telling me about?"

"Yes. There will be a ticket waiting for you under the name Royal Stone."

Royal smiled. It felt good to hear that name again.

He reached out for her hand and kissed it. She did not pull away. She was enchanted by his kindness, grateful for it. He stood back up and looked down into her warm eyes. He could see why Dmitry had left his life for her. She was completely undeniable.

"Please, go," he whispered. "I can't control myself much longer."

Royal smiled and turned to grab the dress bag and jewelry. "Well, thank you again for being such a gentleman," she said in a low voice.

He saw her out and closed the door, aching to have her right then.

Chapter 17

By the time that Royal left Dorian's hotel room, she didn't feel like going back to the boutique. She was mentally exhausted from the thought of having to save her entire family, broken-hearted by her husband's deceitful little secret and confused by her immediate attraction to her husband's arch enemy. Overall, it had been one hell of a morning, so she decided to catch a cab to the condo in town and rest there for a while.

No one would know the difference, but at least she could get a plan in place to get to Sochi without Dmitry knowing.

The clouds had begun to blot out the sun, and the winds started to pick up. It was about to rain. Just what she needed. Raising her hand, she hailed a taxi and hurriedly got out of the weather.

When she got to her condo, she paid the driver and ran out of the rain up to the gate and punched in the code.

As soon as she opened the front door to her home, she knew someone else had been there. She pulled the gun from her purse and proceeded in. After many years of being a Medlov, the one thing she knew was to keep a weapon handy.

Not bothering to say a word, she walked through the house quietly to each room, all of which had been occupied since she had last been there.

At the base of the stairs, she looked up towards the window on the second floor and saw no one in the reflection.

Slowly, she inched up each step until she arrived at the second floor. Her heart pounded a mile a minute in her chest. She swallowed hard as she arrived at her bedroom. The door was open and someone was lying in the bed asleep.

Cocking the gun, she went into the room and nearly fainted as she saw who was in the bed. That bitch, Victoria! She slipped out of her heels and dove into the bed on top of the startled woman.

"You fucking whore!" Royal screamed, snatching the woman up.

Victoria's body jerked and her eyes popped open to see Royal hit her in the eye with the end of her spiked stiletto. Blood spurted across the silver comforter as the women struggled. Royal reached back with a balled up fist and punched Victoria in the lip, then dug her nails into her chest.

"Get off me!"Victoria fought back, but Royal was much too angry and heavy. Her attempts were feeble at most.

Royal dragged her out of the bed by her hair and pointed the gun at her.

"So, Dmitry just figured he would play me like a fucking fiddle, huh? Move you across town like I wouldn't find out? I will cut his balls off!"

"No! No, Anatoly brought me here," she explained, covering her bloody face. "Please!"

"Anatoly?" Royal wiped her tear-stained face.

"He drugged me and brought me here," Victoria explained. "I'm working for him now. I swear!"

Royal stopped pointing the gun, pushed Victoria down and paced from side to side.

"I don't believe you. What the hell would he want with you?"

"I'm supposed to go to Sochi tomorrow."

The words rang in Royal's ears.

"Sochi?"

"Yes," Victoria covered her wounded face. "Dmitry had nothing to do with it!"

"I told you if I ever saw you again..." Royal pointed the gun and screamed. "You fucking home wreaker!"

"I know! I had every intention of leaving. Please. You have to believe me!" the woman cried. "Anatoly wouldn't let me. He grabbed me at the restaurant and brought me here. I don't even know where I am."

"What is going on in my family?" Royal screamed. She put her hand on her head and grunted. She looked back at Victoria bundled up by the bed covering her face. "What are you doing in Sochi tomorrow?"

"Buying art," she stuttered.

"For Dmitry and Anatoly?"

"I guess. I don't know. I wasn't told everything."

"Anatoly brought you here?"

"Yes. See, I'm in his shirt," she looked up at Royal desperately. "He just left. He said he wouldn't be back tonight. I'm supposed to get on a flight in the morning for Sochi and purchase some art tomorrow night. That's all I know."

Royal calmed herself. She breathed through her mouth, exhaling her anger. "You low down, conniving bitch."

"Look, I know that I was wrong," she wiped her face and calmed her breathing. "I've been apologizing for two fucking days, but I think that I've been paid back adequately for what I've done now."

"Did Anatoly touch you?"

"He didn't hurt me if that's what you mean."

"So you slept with him?"

"Yes," she said sighing. "Yes. Okay. I slept with him." She wiped her face on the sleeve of the shirt and shook her head.

Royal looked at her and shook her head in disgust. "I trusted you," she pointed the gun again.

"I. Am. Sorry."

Royal bit her lip and wiped the tears from her face. "Well, sorry just isn't good enough anymore," she said in a cool tone.

Royal leaned against the bed holding her heart and slid down against the mattress. Crying, she let out a painful sob as she dropped the gun.

Victoria was mortified, dumbfounded by what she had done to the woman. She went to her and sat by her on the floor.

"I am sorry," Victoria said in a hushed one.

"Yeah, me too."

They sat quietly in the now silent room alone together.

***

Dmitry had only made it home a half hour before he got a call from a manager at the Hotel Iron Gate. Royal had hand-delivered a dress to a suite and a gentlemen staying alone by the name of Andrew Oriachiav.

When he hung up the phone, he threw it across the room, knocking the picture off the wall. He knew something was wrong with Royal. It had to be this *Andrew* guy. Royal never hand-delivered a damned thing. And she was so eager to leave the restaurant earlier with her story about the shop.

He stood up and paced the room for a minute, turning redder by the second. If she was cheating on him with another man, he would kill her lover right in front of her. He would cut his heart out of his body and cut it into pieces in front of her! He leaned against the desk, then threw all the contents against the wall.

"Davyd!" he called, pulling his guns out of his desk drawer. "Bring my fucking car around and get the men together!"

***

Royal and Victoria talked over a cup of coffee and an emergency kit that Royal used to apply to Victoria wounds. They discussed the deal and Victoria's brief sexual encounter with Anatoly. Oddly enough, Royal had been extremely understanding and forgiving of the woman.

"I need your help, Victoria," Royal said, applying a bandage.

"How?"

"I have money. Lots of it. I need to get to Sochi with you in the morning. Don't tell anyone – especially Anatoly."

"What if the flight is full?

"Have you ever offered a flight attendant a thousand bucks to move things around? It works. Trust me."

"So, if you go to Sochi, you plan to do what?"

"Save my family. I'm the only one who can. Dorian won't trust or listen to anyone else. Tell you the truth, I'm not sure why he would even listen to me."

Victoria sighed. "Do you think it's a set up?"

"This is going to sound really crazy, but...no, I don't. I looked into his eyes, listened to what he had to say, and I truly believe him. Now, if I'm wrong, then we're all dead. But if I'm right, I could be the only thing standing between a war that could kill us all."

Victoria thought Royal was really brave and selfless for her concern. "Okay. I'll do it, but I don't know if it will work."

Royal smiled. "Thank you."

"Can you ever forgive me, Royal, for being such a horrible person?"

"I'm surrounded by horrible people. Yes, I can forgive you, especially if you help me save my boys."

Royal's cell phone range. She looked down. It was Dmitry.

"Does he know that you're here?" Royal asked Victoria.

"I don't know. I don't' think so."

"Okay." She answered her phone. "Hi, honey." She tried to sound like nothing was wrong.

"Where are you?" he asked..

"I'm out in the city. Why?"

"You're supposed to be at work. You're not. I'm here waiting on you, and you haven't been back since you picked up dress."

Royal huffed. "Why are you checking on me?" That was most unlike Dmitry. He was never the smothering type.

"Why should I have to check on you? Where are you?" his voice raised.

"In. The. City." She snapped.

"You better not be at that fucking hotel with this Andrew."

Royal was shocked. "I'm not. I'm headed to the restaurant not far from our condo across town.   Meet me there, if you want, in a few minutes."

"Are you lying to me?"

"No, I'm not lying to you, Dmitry. Goodness! You sound insane."

"You have no idea," he hung up the phone.

"I don't think he knows where you are," Royal said to Victoria. "I have to go. I can't let him know that I know about tomorrow, no matter what."

Royal rushed out of the house after calling a taxi and Dorian.   Hearing the news, Dorian immediately left the hotel through service entrance and headed for his plane. He had to get out of town before Dmitry found him.

Chapter 18

Within minutes, Royal was sitting at the bar of the pub down the street from her condo awaiting Dmitry. He barged into the restaurant alone with guns visible looking for her with a scowl on his face covered in rain water. His clothes stuck to his body and revealed the tattoos he hid underneath.

Royal sat up in the bar stool and pulled her hair behind her ear. Goodness. He looked psychotic. The veins stuck out of his neck and his face was red with anger. He eyed her as he walked up, looking as if he would strike her.

"Why are you here?" he asked, staring at her with an irate grimace. "And not at work?"

"What is your problem, Dmitry? You're acting like a mad man."

"Don't lie to me."

"I'm not lying."

Grabbing her wrist, he pulled her out of the chair and dragged her out of the bar screaming and kicking. The few onlookers did not intervene. Instead they watched the giant man in amazement. He carried her in one arm into the rain where Davyd stood waiting.

When he tried to put her in his Bentley, she reached up and slapped him as hard as she could in his face.

"You fucking bastard!" she screamed as he placed her inside.

Jumping in the front seat, he ordered Davyd to pull off into the rainy streets. "I'm the bastard?"

"Yes!"

"What the hell were you doing at some other man's hotel room?"

"Why are you spying on me?"

"I'm not. I got a call...."

"Fuck you! You get to cheat with whores under my roof," she pushed her finger against her chest, "and I go and deliver a damned dress, and you treat me like I'm some corner rat!"

"I didn't cheat."

"I saw you kiss her, Dmitry. You were hard as hell. You wanted to fuck her in my house!"

"I wanted to kill her in *your* house! There is a difference!" He looked over his seat at her.

"I have had it up to here with you!" she touched her forehead. "You and all your bullshit. If I were a man, I would kick your ass!"

"Who was he? I went by the hotel, and he had already gone. A fucking coward. Little does he know that my reach is much farther than this city. I'll find him, whether you tell me who he is or not."

"I don't know who he is. He bought a fucking dress! Do you know how many dresses I sell a week?"

"The same dress that the manager said you brought back downstairs with you?" Dmitry ignored the rest of her rant.

"He said he changed his mind!"

"After he got what he really wanted. I would change my mind, too!"

"Fuck you. You think you run the entire world. You don't run shit. You don't run me. And for the last time, I didn't do anything!" Royal instantly thought of Victoria pleading with her one the hour before regarding her innocence. It was hard to be the accused.

Dmitry paused. He had never in his existence with Royal ever had a man once intrude on his territory. The thought of another man being with her infuriated him beyond his control. But there was the sobering thought that Royal was a true lady and had never once faltered.

Then there was the thought of revenge. He had kissed Victoria among other things in clear view and unknowingly in front of Royal. Why wouldn't she seek revenge? Women always sought revenge. His blood boiled. He wanted to kill. He wanted to rip the man's throat out with his bare hands.

He looked back at his wife, tear-stained and wide-eyed. She was telling the truth, but still he could not control his anger.

Davyd looked over at him with concern. This had gotten completely out of control. He had never seen Dmitry so angry with Royal. Because of his relationship with her, he wanted to step in and say something, but he knew Dmitry's temper. It could cost them all more than it could save anyone.

Dmitry looked over at Davyd with pure rage in his eyes. Royal was his everything. Without her and Anya, he had nothing. He would not lose her without a serious fight, one that lasted until the death. She did not know that he had seen the video of the man who she had delivered the dress to earlier that day. She did not know that Andrew was actually Dorian, his arch enemy from many years ago – a true brother to Ivan.

Yet, he had taken everything out on her as if she did know. Fury had gripped him, paralyzed him from rational thought. It was shameful, the way that he had treated her.

Royal sat in the back seat with tears in her eyes and her arms folded. Looking out the window, she gritted her teeth and talked under her breath.

When they pulled into the garage of their home, she opened the door and darted into the house, still cursing at Dmitry.

"You messed up," Davyd said to Dmitry.

"*Da Da.* I know, *brat.*"

"Better go to her before she has time to think too much. You know how she can be."

Dmitry ran after her, following her through the long corridor, up the stairs to the second floor.

First thing first, Royal checked in on Anya. She had fallen asleep in the TV room watching a movie with her doll on the floor.

Royal picked her up and carried her to her bedroom with Dmitry following like her shadow.

"I'm sorry," he whispered behind her.

"Whatever," Royal snapped. "Open the door," she ordered at Anya's bedroom door.

He twisted the knob and moved out of her way.

Whisking past, Royal laid Anya in the bed and covered her up.

"We need to talk," Dmitry whispered again.

"Go to hell," she said, leaving the room.

Stomping down to her room, she opened the door and tried to slam it behind her, but Dmitry caught it and pushed in. She turned around and stared at him.

"You fucking bastard," she said in a low growl.

"Don't you dare talk to me like that," he said walking closer. His voice was low and stern.

"Or what? You'll kill me too?" Her cat-like eyes narrowed.

"No," he said incensed. "I messed up. Alright. My head is still screwed up because of Victoria."

"Don't you dare speak her name in this bedroom."

"What else am I supposed to call her?"

She rolled her eyes. "What has gotten into you, Dmitry? You know that I would never allow a man to treat me the way that you just did. I am not one of your *belongings*. Okay. I have my own mind and my own rights. I don't owe you, of all people, an explanation. If you don't trust me, then fine. Leave me. But don't go accusing me, because you are perverted." She rolled her eyes.

Dmitry breathed in hard. "I. Said. I. Was. Sorry."

"Tell me what's going on with you. If you just told me, I could understand better. I could forgive you," she pleaded.

Dmitry bottled up. "Nothing is wrong. I thought something that was not so."

"Nothing is going on?" she asked with her hands on her hips.

"No."

Royal huffed. He still chose to lie even when it would have benefited him just to tell her the truth, which was that he had gone back to the Vory.

"I think that you should sleep in the guest room tonight," she bit out.

"I'm not sleeping in the guest room tonight or any other night," he growled. The veins showed in his neck again.

"This is a marriage bed, and people who are married tell each other the truth," she lectured.

"What do you want me to say, *zhenshchina*!?"

"Just tell me the truth!" she cried.

"There is nothing wrong!" he snarled, turning from her. He walked to the door and was about to leave when he saw her head to the closet. He turned around quickly and followed her.

"Are you looking for valium? I threw it all away," he said. He rounded the corner to find her pulling a nightgown from her dresser.

"You really are a bastard," she said with tears in her eyes. "I made a promise, didn't I?"

He paused in shock, wishing instantly he could take back his words.

She walked past him, but he caught her arm in the fold and pulled her to him.

"Let me go!" she screamed.

Effortlessly, he snatched her up in his arms and felt her slap him again across his face again. He carried her kicking and screaming to the bed. She fell back on it and cried.

"I hate you. You're a liar!"

Dmitry caught her hand as she tried to swing again. He pulled her to him and held her down on the bed. It was déjà vu and also very much like a horrid fight that they had in Memphis many years ago.

"You BASTARD!" she roared.

"Call me what you want to call me, but I am your husband, provider of your lifestyle and head of this house! I have the right to be concerned...*territorial even*. What did you expect me to do? Do you think that I have grown so soft that I would just let another man come in a steal you? I am still the same man I was when you met me. I have not changed who I am, just my tactics." He looked her in her eyes as he spoke with authority and sheer anger.

"Am I supposed to be impressed with that?"

"I would kill him. I would kill anyone who dare got in my way, even Davyd or Anatoly. And I would enjoy it."

Royal gasped. He was a monster!

"I'm not as strong as you, Royal. I couldn't take it if you cheated on me or left me for another man. I could not allow it."

"I didn't cheat," Royal said again with tears in her eyes. "I have never cheated on you. Why are you so insecure?"

"I don't know." Dmitry let her hands go and deflated against her. "I felt in my heart that something inappropriate had happened. I could not control my rage."

"Don't you think I know by now that you're crazy? Why would I even do that to another person – put them in a position to have to deal with you? I delivered a damned dress. He changed his mind. I left. No big deal."

"It is very big deal to me."

"Everything is a very big deal to you," her voice was soft. Royal put her hands on his head.

He bent over and rested on her stomach, sighing as he did so. He just couldn't bring himself to tell her that he had put her in harm's way again.

"Dmitry, you're heavy," Royal said, pushing his concrete body up off of her. "Get up."

He raised his head a little and grunted, then ran his large hands down her torso to the button of her skirt.

Royal looked down as he moved quietly. She felt her clothes being pulled off. Her skirt. Her stockings. Her shoes.

He stood on the side of the bed and pulled her body to him. Without uttering a word, he picked her hips up off the bed and tasted her.

"Dmitry, I need to take a shower," she protested, trying to pull away. Though the feeling was all pleasure, she couldn't help but feel a little embarrassment. Every woman liked to shower first.

Dmitry ignored her. He focused, apologizing through his silent actions.

Royal looked up at the ceiling in a daze as she finally gave in to his kisses. Her long black hair spilled like oil across the bed as her body convulsed slowly against his tongue.

She bit her lip and curled her fingers as his hot breath brushed her skin. His mouth nearly covered her mound. The suction created a warm flutter from within her. Like petals blooming in spring, she began to open up. Approvingly, he continued to move at an erotically sensual pace.

"I'm..." she tried to breathe. "I'm...." The words refused to form on her tongue as she climaxed.

She heard Dmitry's pants hit the floor and felt her body shift. With one move, he had her on her knees in the soft bed. With another move, he buried himself deep inside of her. The extreme impact caused goose bumps to form on her body. So heavy, so big, so good. Her mouth watered as she heard him give a deep growl. As he pulled away, she let out a grateful sigh. Then with an angry thrust, he returned to the depths of her. She cried out.

"I'm sorry," he whispered in her ear as he held her close. "I didn't want tonight to be like this, my love."

Royal didn't answer. She couldn't. She clenched her teeth together and held on to the bedpost as a warm wave started to come over her again as he moved in a rhythmic motion back and forth.

He moved her hair out of way and kissed her neck. Closing her eyes, she moaned. Reaching back, she grabbed his vein-filled, muscular arm gripping her waist and pushed back into him.

"Yes," he said as he felt her pressure.

Opening her legs wider, she did it again.

"Yes," he said in a more strained baritone.

She finally opened her legs as far as they could separate, lifted her hips, pulled away and bucked against him as hard as she could for several minutes. He countered every stroke with his own.

"Fuck," Dmitry bit out in strained voice, spilling his seed into her. He pulled her close into his powerful embrace and pushed deep into her.

His potent thrusts were almost too much for Royal, even after many years of being his wife. She grabbed the comforter as her body jerked. Closing her eyes, the wave of heat that she tried to fight off, came back, this time more powerful than ever. Her body began to shake as she climaxed again. She finally screamed out loud enough to hear down the hallways.

"Oh, Dmitry!"

Chapter 19

After dinner with Anya, Dmitry, Davyd and Anatoly that evening, Royal slipped into her study and called Victoria. Before Royal left the condo earlier that day, Victoria had given her two pills that she promised would incapacitate Davyd until they were out of the country in the morning. She only hoped their little plan worked.

"Hello."

"Victoria?"

"Yeah. It's me. Did you get in trouble?"

"Sort of. I could have sworn that he knew, but he thought that I was cheating."

"Guilt, I guess."

"Yeah. Are you sure these pills are going to work?"

"Oh, they'll work. Just open them and pour them into Davyd's coffee in the morning. He'll be out like a light."

"I don't want to hurt him."

"You won't. They're harmless in moderation."

"Okay. Well, I'll call you in the morning right before I give them to him. I called Brigitte when

I got home. She'll pick you up and make sure you get inside the gate."

"Okay. I'll be waiting."

Royal hung up the phone and took a deep breath. Never in all her life had she done so much conniving in such a short period of time. She felt like a dirty little spy, but the alternative was to let her family die, and she couldn't do that.

Dmitry knocked on the door and opened it. He leaned against the entry and yawned.

"What are you doing in here?"

"Work. I have a lot to do tomorrow." She smiled a little, realizing that she wasn't really lying. "What about you? I saw Brigitte packing your bags."

Dmitry paused. "I have a follow-up meeting in Sochi tomorrow. I'll return home day after tomorrow."

"Can I go?"

Dmitry raised his brow. "This is very boring meeting with very boring men. You won't enjoy yourself."

"I'll take that as a no," she said, typing on her computer.

"Trust me. I'm doing you a favor." He tried to sound upbeat and playful.

Royal hated when he lied. She tried to bite her tongue and control her heating temper. "What time do you leave in the morning?"

"Early."

"Well, since you'll be gone, Anatoly can help do a few things at the shop.   I need a man's opinion."

"He's going with me."   He looked her in her eyes.

"Anatoly? Why?"

Dmitry scratched his five o'clock shadow as he lied. "I think he has girl in Sochi."

"Oh. Okay," she smiled. "Well, goodnight."

"You're not coming to bed?"

"I'm going to stop and check on Anya first, then maybe I'll be there."

"Alright.   Don't stay up too long.   Good night."

"Night," Royal said, watching him close her door. She rolled her eyes when she heard his feet head down the corridor. "Liar," she mouthed as she closed her laptop.

In less than a half an evening, she had conceived a master plan to save the very man who would rather die than tell her truth, beat the woman who tried to screw him and seen a very attractive stranger naked. To say that she had experienced a full day was less than explanatory. She was surprised that she was still sane and valium-free.

A small grin crossed her pierced lips. She was sort of proud of herself too. This was more excitement than she had had in her life for three years.

***

In the morning, at the crack of dawn, Royal felt Dmitry stir beside her. He looked up at the ceiling with his hands behind his head thinking for a while and then reached over to see if she was awake.

She kept her breathing calm, even when he whispered her name and sank his lips into her neck to kiss her. His breath sent tingles down her skin and his tongue electrified her. It was impossible for her to keep her moans to herself when his large hand ran over her body, but she always did that in her sleep. He was never the wiser.

"Are you sleeping so hard that you can't wake for me?" Dmitry asked, pulling up her gown. "I need you this morning. I need my *Royal Flush*."

His fingers trailed down the side of her thighs up to her abdomen and cupped her breasts. When she did not respond, he sighed heavily.

"Please understand that the only reason that I'm doing this is for the family. It's not for me," he confessed as he kissed the back of her head. "If I don't protect you, who will?" His words were more for himself than her.

Royal held back tears and clenched her eyes closed. She did not move though she wanted to reach out to him and hold him tight. She felt his large body embrace her from behind. The heat from his skin was against her own. His rigid, concrete muscles wrapped around her, and she found herself even with her eyes closed completely lost. She bit her lip and buried her face in the pillow to keep the torture from getting to her. How much more of this could she take?

"I love you," Dmitry said finally.

He pushed the comforter from his legs and got out of bed.

In the darkness of the room, Royal watched his massive, naked frame disappear into the bathroom and close the door. She rolled over in the bed, in his spot, in his heat and sighed. His cologne lingered on his pillow. She inhaled him and felt her heart skip a beat. *My Dmitry*, she thought to herself, *I love you, too*.

***

When she was certain that Dmitry's helicopter had picked both himself and Anatoly up, Royal jumped out of bed and ran to the shower a little more than an hour later.

Where she normally took forever to get dolled up, she only took minutes to run through the water, brush her teeth and wash her face. With no makeup and no jewelry, she pulled on a pair of jeans, a turtleneck and gym shoes and headed downstairs.

"Momma said she was going to take me to Disneyland one day, Davyd," Anya said, eating her cereal at the kitchen table as she watched the Disney Channel.

"I'm sure she did. Don't talk with your mouth full, darling," Davyd admonished.

"She can take you, too," Anya added.

"I've already been," Davyd smiled at Anya and put his hand over her small mouth. "Now, no talking with *your mouth full.*"

"Good morning," Royal said, entering the room with a bright smile.

"Good morning, Mommy," Anya greeted.

"Morning," Davyd looked on curiously. "You don't...don't look like yourself this morning in the jeans and everything. You look, I don't know, like you're 17."

Royal smiled, taking his observation as a compliment. "Well, I'm going to really get the back room of the boutique clean today. So, I figured that I better dress down."

Davyd nodded. "Dmitry gave me direct orders that you were not to go near the boutique today."

"Dmitry should have been man enough to give his orders to me then," she said with her hand on her hips. "I'm going."

Davyd didn't say a word. He didn't have to. Royal knew that if it were up to him, she would not get out of the house today.

"Would you like a cup of coffee?" Royal asked, finally trying to calm her bear of a bodyguard.

"I've already had two cups this morning."

"Have another with me. I want to talk to you."

"Alright. Pour me another," he passed her his mug.

Royal took the cup with a polite smile and ran her hand through Anya's hair.

"Mommy, didn't you say that we could go to Disneyworld some day?" Anya asked.

"*Someday*, darling."

"Why not now?"

"Because papa and I don't go to the states," Royal said, pouring Davyd's cup of coffee. She turned with her back to both of them, opened the capsules and dumped them into his cup. She looked back and smiled to make sure no one was looking. They were not.

Why would they not trust me, Royal thought to herself.

"Anya, honey, are you finished eating?" Royal asked.

"Yes," Anya answered.

"*Yes*, what?"

"Yes, ma'am," Anya said with a smile.

"Well then run into the great room and sit there while I talk *big talk* with Davyd."

Anya got up and ran out with Davyd's eyes following her as she did. Royal quickly fixed the other cup of coffee with creamer and sugar and returned to the table.

She sat down across from him and put her hands on her cheeks.

"You watch that girl like a hawk," she observed.

"I have to watch both of you like hawk. You're both always up to something. Speaking of which, what are you so happy about today?" Davyd asked, sipping his coffee.

"I wouldn't say that I am so much happy as I am eager."

"About what?"

"I was hoping you could tell me what Dmitry and Anatoly are doing in Sochi." She fluttered her long lashes and gave a sarcastic grin.

Her charm didn't work.

"Why didn't you ask them?" David grunted.

"So they could lie to me," she smirked. "When I can ask you and get the truth, why bother?"

"I don't know what they're doing in Sochi," he said yawning.

"Has he returned to the Vory?" she asked seriously.

Davyd frowned. "No."

"I don't believe you."

"Then ask *him*."

Davyd said something in Russian under his breath and pulled at the collar of his polo. "Is it hot in here to you, or is it just me?"

"It's warm," Royal said, scooting away from her seat. She eyed him. *Was it already working?*

"Let's go into the study, I want to show you something I found that made me think that Dmitry was going back," she said.

Davyd's pensive lips curved around his words. "Now listen to me, Royal, you know better than to snoop."

"I wasn't snooping," she said calmly. "Just...come with me. Goodness, you look peaked."

"I feel faint." He looked down at his empty coffee cup. "Did you put something in my cup?

"Don't be ridiculous. Who do I look like to you, Victoria?"

Davyd growled. "Sorry, dear. We're all on edge lately."

"That's okay. Here. Let me help you."

Royal went and helped him up, guided him to the great room, over to his favorite recliner and sat him down.

Before she could go and get a towel to wipe his sweaty forehead, he had passed out.

Anya walked over to Davyd and pulled on his large fingers to wake him as he lay unconscious in the chair.

"Why is he sleeping again already?" Anya looked up at her mother with bright blue eyes.

Royal thought of Ivan but worked past it. "He's tired, honey. Now stay in here until Brigitte get's here. She's going to watch you until Mommy and Daddy get back."

"Where are you and Daddy going?"

She knew better than to tell her daughter the truth. Anya would just tell Davyd when he woke. "Mommy's going to town for the garden," she said cleverly.

"Can I go?"

"No. Stay here and watch Davyd."

"Okay."

Royal went to the DVD player, put on an animated movie and left her daughter on the couch.

By the time that she got to her study, she heard footsteps down the hall.

She peaked out quickly. It was Brigitte and Victoria. She opened the door and waved them in.

"Hurry," she ordered, looking down the hallway to make sure that no one had seen them.

They ran into the office and closed the door behind them.

"Brigitte, when I've gone, run to the security room and get rid of the footage from this morning. Watch Anya and wait for us to call. If Dmitry calls, tell him that I'm on in the garden with the gardeners again and have plans to be on the land all day."

"*Oui*, Madame," Brigitte said, confused but willing to help.

"Victoria, how long will David be out?" Royal asked.

"It's hard to say, but it'll be a while," Victoria whispered.

Royal shook her head. "Briggy, when Davyd wakes up, tell him that he must have gotten sick. Wash the cups out in the kitchen; make sure there is no evidence. He won't call Dmitry until he's certain that he can't find me. Tell him that I was out in the garden and then I left and went into the town for flowers. I'm leaving my cell phone here. Tell him, I must have forgotten it."

"What if he..." Brigitte worried.

"Tell him you don't know anything else. He'll believe you. It's damned near true."

"Alright," Brigitte said with her hands clasped together. "Good Luck."

"Thanks. And thank you for your help. I couldn't do this without you. Victoria, we'd better go, quickly," Royal said, taking a deep breath. "Let's pray that this works."

They grabbed the bags and headed towards the garage.

Chapter 20

Dmitry and Anatoly arrived in Sochi to a large entourage of their men, who already had been instructed to get Russia immediately. Over fifty men were strategically placed around the city, many of them at the airport. Even Anatoly had to take note of his father's flawless execution.

Dmitry was all business today. He went over the plan twice with his son on the plane, sent his top guys to prepare their teams for the possibility of an ambush, had the lawyers on call and was strapped like a black ops solider under his perfectly cut suit.

After seeing that Dorian had not only been in Prague but had interaction with his wife, he had activated a team in Prague, Sochi, Memphis, and Moscow. They could not be too careful now. He knew Dorian well, and if there was one thing he was good at, it was the element of surprise. Only this time, he'd be ready for him.

In watching his father, Anatoly realized that he still had so much to learn from the real boss. With his father, they moved with finesse and accuracy from one location to the other on time and seamlessly, even with their large numbers.

Dmitry had explained to Anatoly earlier that there was nothing more dangerous than closing a deal, even in the most public of places. And with the kind of money that they were dealing with tonight, there would be a need for a small army.

"Load them into different cars," said Dmitry's bodyguard as he routed the men.

"See you at the hotel," Dmitry said to Anatoly as he loaded in the back of his car with his men.

"Alright, let's go," Anatoly said, following his bodyguards to his car.

***

Dorian sat at the dinner table with the only representative from the Spentznas that would actively participate in the deal. The older man seemed relaxed and at peace. He ate his lobster slowly, relishing in the taste and occasionally sipping his wine.

Dorian found it odd that he drank wine and ate lobster when their restaurant served the best Beluga caviar in the city. But it was of no consequence to him.

"I trust everything is on schedule," the man said, dapping his weathered, tanned mouth with the napkin.

"Yes, it is," Dorian answered without looking up to make eye contact with the man.

"And the Medlov's are still prepared to buy?"

Dorian smiled casually as looked up from his plate. Although he inwardly cringed at someone second guessing his ability to coordinate a buy, he played along. He knew the line of questioning was going somewhere.

"They will be here tonight at the masquerade ball. We'll meet briefly in a side room, where we will go undetected after their person purchases the art at the art show across town," he answered.

"I did a little checking on the Medlov's and found out that you have had dealings with them before, at least on the occasion when Dmitry tried to kill you." The man raised his brow and put down his napkin.

"All water under the bridge."

"I have worked in Intel for 25 years. I've seen my country turn from a dictatorship to a democracy. I know that there is no such thing as *water under the bridge.*"

"Well, let's just say that our past relationship won't interfere with the deal. You'll be on your way *with* your money before there is ever even a word uttered."

"Good. Well then, you'll have your final fee tonight, and my colleagues and I will be on our way to a pleasant retirement."

"I'll toast to that," Dorian said, raising his glass of water.

**

When Royal and Victoria arrived in Sochi, they headed directly to the hotel where Anatoly had reserved a room for Victoria to dress before the art show. Hidden in plain sight, Royal blended in to the thousands of people rushing through the city going back and forth to the Winter Olympic Games.

She was amazed at all the activity and had not seen so many people crowded in one central location in her life. It was exhilarating for her to move on her own, make her own decisions and most of all to be unescorted for once. There was no entourage, no men with guns, no limos and diamonds – just her with a backpack and a dress bag.

She smiled to herself as the people zoomed by her, brushing against her, ignoring her – not fearing her like they often did when they saw the Medlov clan parading through a city.

However, when they arrived, she saw that being a Medlov had its perks and not being with her husband had its drawbacks. Checking into the hotel was actually more complicated than she had first thought.

All the rooms where booked, her money wasn't good enough to bump anyone out and to announce that she was Dmitry's Medlov's wife would send alarms off to all the wrong people.

"No big deal. You can just stay in my room," Victoria said, taking her key card from the hotel desk clerk.

"That's probably not smart," Royal sighed. "Anatoly will surely come to see you before you go."

"Why would he?"

Royal raised her brow. "You don't know the Medlov men very well, do you? He'll come up before he goes to make the deal and pick up where he left off. *Probably a quickie.* But one thing's for sure. He'll come to you."

Victoria hadn't thought of that.

"Well, what will you do?" she asked, looking around the elaborate lobby perplexed. "There's probably not a hotel in the city that isn't booked."

She looked at her watch. "I have four hours. I'll get across town, find a hovel somewhere that's not on the tourist grid, and I'll make my way back here by show time. Do you have your phone on?"

"Yeah, you got your throw away?"

"Yeah."

"Okay, well good luck. We probably won't see each other before this all goes down."

Royal felt compelled. She paused and then reached out and hugged her. "Thanks for helping me."

"Thanks for asking. Anatoly didn't give me a choice with the other part." She pushed Royal's long black ponytail from her shoulder and rubbed her arm. "Take care of yourself, Royal."

Royal shook her head. "You too." She adjusted her backpack and headed out of the hotel into the streets of the city to catch a cab.

***

Davyd saw flashes of light as he came to. His eyes fluttered, and he realized that he was sitting in the chair with his feet elevated in the great room. Anya sat on his lap watching television and *doing his hair*, which consisted of a lot mousse and colorful barrettes.

He cleared his voice and shifted her off his left leg that had gone to sleep. Patting her back, he beckoned her to move.

"Up, up, Anya," he growled.

As bolt of lightning stuck through him as he noticed that it was nightfall and felt the sweat on his back. How long had he been asleep?

He looked down at his watch and realized that it was a quarter past ten. Jumping up, he dashed out of the room, screaming for Stepan and Brigitte.

"Where is everyone? Stepan! Briggy!"

His old bones rattled as he moved as fast as he could.

Stepan came down the hall with guns on his side and four men following behind him. Davyd instantly recognized them. They were men from Dmitry's small army in Prague. If they had been activated, then something was wrong. He straightened his pants and wiped his sweaty face.

"Where is Royal?" he asked, knowing without being told that she was not there.

"That is what we have been trying to find out. Brigitte swears that she went into town. But *you* were unconscious, and we haven't seen her all day. Plus, she hasn't been to shop."

"Has Dmitry been notified?"

"Of course." Stepan clenched his jaw. He knew protocol.

"What did he say?"

"He said if she wasn't here then she was there. He's sent a team to comb the streets and look for her in Sochi."

Davyd hit the wall with his fist and felt for his guns. They had been taken. Probably by Royal. Stepan looked at him in his frustration and looked back at the men. "We took your guns. Didn't want Anya to shoot you in your sleep." They all smirked at the older man.

"Well give them back and give me a few men. We're headed to Sochi," he growled.

"Dmitry said you'd say that. He said that what is done can't be undone now. He wants everyone here with Anya, just in case. Call him if you like. He has got over a hundred men on the premises here in trees and out in the barn, throughout the house. You name it. We're on lockdown until whatever is happening *happens*."

"Well if that's the case, then send ten men into great room. We'll sit with Anya until Dmitry arrives back to this house with Royal. Send man to the insides and outsides of every exit and tell them to take their safeties off." He started to walk off. "And give me my fucking guns back."

***

Full dressed in a tailored tuxedo, Dmitry sat in his suite with his son drinking a glass of vodka in the silent calm of luxurious ambience. Everything was ready, and now it was time to wait.

Anatoly watched his father carefully. Something was off. Clearing his voice, he broke the silence and uncrossed his legs.

Dmitry looked up from his distant thoughts and peered at Anatoly under blonde eyelashes. He moved the glass from his hand. The dim lights flickered off of the diamonds in his Rolex.

"I'm sure that they'll find her," Anatoly assured his father.

They had only found out a couple of hours earlier than Royal was missing. Dmitry was silent when he first found out. The wheels of his mind turned over and over until he finally spoke, informing them all that she was in the city. Anatoly found it odd, almost impossible. How did she find out? But Dmitry was certain and if he was certain, even if he was wrong, in their world it was the truth.

"Let me worry about Royal," Dmitry said finally. He smiled revealing his long, deep dimples. His eyes sparkled. "Victoria should be preparing to go over to the art gallery to make the final payment. Has she been properly instructed?"

"Yes." Anatoly sat up in the chair a little straighter. Would his father ever stop grilling him?

"You know, if you care for her at all, you should send one of the other men?"

"Care for her?" Anatoly smirked. "I told you..."

"Listen to me. You send pawns out in the field – people who you do not care if they don't come back. You don't send anyone you care about."

"Papa, she'll be fine."

Dmitry didn't smile. His voice was low. "No one is safe tonight, especially anyone involved in *this* deal. She could go to jail. She could be kidnapped. She could be killed. Are you ready to accept that?"

"She'll be fine," Anatoly stood up and walked over to the window. He looked out at all the people moving around on the streets below. It was like New Years in New York.

"You don't have much time to change your mind," he heard Dmitry say from behind him. His voice sounded worried – worried about a woman who had betrayed him and his wife.

"My mind is made up."

"Moving on then," Dmitry put down his glass on the table beside his chair and planted his elbows on his long legs. "I don't want you at the ball. I need you on the yacht. Once the deal is made, I have a feeling that the only way they're going to get the shipment out of the city is by water."

Anatoly hadn't thought of that, but it sounded like a good idea. He nodded. "Alright." He turned around to face his father.

Dmitry looked at his watch and stood up. "You know regardless of what happens tonight, I am very proud of you, and everything that I've done, I've done for you." His father stood to his full height, revealing the giant he was in stature and life. He gleamed with intelligence, power and success. It was his look that captivated the masses. It was his strength that dominated the underworld.   He walked over his to son and placed his large hands on his shoulders. "If you don't learn anything else from me, I hope you've learned that I've always known what my priorities are."

"I know, Papa. And I appreciate it, from the bottom of my heart," Anatoly said. "Thieves-in-Law."

"Thieves-in-Law," Dmitry said as he let his son go. "Now, go on. Get to it. If God is willing, I'll see you at dawn." He hugged him tight.

"Damn. You're packing heavy, eh?" Anatoly observed feeling the large bulge under his father's clothes.

Dmitry smiled and pointed at the door. The men standing at the door opened it and moved out the way as Anatoly headed out. Dmitry gave his lead man a nod as he watched his son leave.

***

Royal zipped up her long black gown and twisted it around on her body. Adjusting her cleavage, she pulled out the diamonds Dmitry bought her to cover up her scars, placed on her four-carat diamond earrings, slipped on her wedding ring and slipped her credit card and ID inside the corset of her dress.

She had just enough time today to purchase a
gun in the raunchy hourly hotel she was holed up
in almost an hour away from Downtown Sochi.

She had traded her watch and IPod for it.
Totally worth it. She could hear the prostitutes
working in every room around her and the smell
of damp, mildewed walls nearly choked her, but
she breathed it happily knowing that it was to
save her family.

The filth and grime was like second skin to
her. It was only a few short years ago that she
was an orphan in the ghetto of Memphis getting
banged around by men who only wanted to harm
her. This was nothing. This was temporary. In
fact, it fueled her tonight.

Face made up and heels on, she slipped the
gun under her dress, dropped her backpack in the
garbage can and headed out to meet her future.

***

Royal was right, Anatoly showed up like she said
he would at Victoria's hotel door with what
looked like a football team behind him of armed
bodyguards. He came in alone, slipping through
the door in a tuxedo and looking like a million
dollars.

Her breath caught in her throat as he moved
towards her. She didn't remember him looking
quite so handsome. His eyes burned like fire

through her, glimmered like blue waters against a white beach.

"I had to have you," he whispered in a husky growl. "Couldn't wait a second longer."

"Me either," she gasped. "Don't ruin the dress though."

"Fuck the dress."

Slipping his hand behind her head, he pulled her into his kiss – sweet and intoxicating. She could not deny it. In fact, she longed for it, although it had only been a day. She wrapped her arms around him and felt him pick her up as he bruised her mouth with his lips.

Carrying her to the bed in his arms, he had a sly grin on his face. Devious mischief was on his mind. He threw her on the bed and pulled off his jacket, revealing shiny silver guns in their forbidden holsters.

She pulled her dress up to her hips as he reached for her panties. He pulled them off slowly, drinking her body through his eyes. He kissed the folds of her long legs down to her black heels and dropped his pants.

Knees in the bed, he skipped the condom and fell down into the depths of her warmness. She let out a sigh and closed her eyes. Back arched, she felt his cold hands slip behind her and pull her to him. He wanted to feel every part of her body against him.

He grunted as he pushed through her with hard, powerful thrusts. His voice was a rumbling growl as he felt her wet flesh tightened around him. Breathing through her nose, eyeing him as he devoured her, she gripped his firm ass and licked his smooth neck. He bit her, leaving a mark on her shoulder.

A strangled scream erupted as he slipped a hand in between her legs and found her pearl. He brushed against it making her body throb from within. Her body was on fire, burning as he speared into her with eager jolts of lava-like lust. He begged for more as he searched her, probed her body as sensations of climatic eruptions began. Suddenly, she hoped this wouldn't be a quickie.

Chapter 21

Victoria's job was the first wave of the deal. After she had freshened up, she headed out of the hotel with a small entourage behind her. For once, she could understand the haughtiness that Royal picked up living this kind of lifestyle.

All eyes were on her as she walked in a convoy of good looking, well-dressed mafiya men, escorting her through the crowd to the limo awaiting her at the door. She had an adrenaline high before she made to the lobby.

People moved out of her way as she passed. They looked curiously. She could see them whispering to their friends. "Who is that? Is she famous?" She could hear them say. *Yeah, bitches, I am*, she thought to herself. A small grin crossed her glossed lips as she lifted her head little higher.

Two motorcycles led the limo and two followed it. She sat back in her seat as her heartbeat raced with excitement.

Her thoughts went back to Royal for a moment. She hoped that she was okay, but Royal had told her not to call unless something was wrong. So far, everything was going right. She looked out the window at the foreign city and bright lights.

When she arrived at the art gallery, the mood changed. Suddenly, she was not the only star. There were so many limos lined outside of the posh, upscale building until she couldn't count them.

People stood outside in formal gowns and tuxedos and bodyguards stood by the cars with earpieces in their ears. The man in the front of the limo looked back at her, then got out and opened the door for her.

She swallowed hard and got out. Escorted through the crowd, she clutched her purse and flashed her invitation as the doors opened for her. A tall blonde woman was waiting for her. She had very distinct Russian accent.

Smiling, she lifted her left hand and motioned towards the back. They walked pass all the crowds, down a long, dimly light corridor all the way to the back to a room guarded by huge white bodyguards peering at her with an evil stare.

The men moved out of her way as she and her men entered the room. She was glad for her bodyguards as she looked around. There was only one piece of art. No artist. No crowd. No people. A single computer sat on a small black table in front of the bust that Victoria assumed was the $550,000,000.00 art.

"Please come this way," the woman said, walking up to the computer. She lifted the monitor and smiled. "Enter you account number here and then...we wait."

"Alright," Victoria said, taking a deep breath.

She walked over the computer and carefully put the numbers that Anatoly had made her commit to memory in. She heard the click of her nails against the keyboard. When she was finished, she folded her arms against her and looked over at her bodyguards.

The blonde woman stepped in front of the computer, typed something very quickly into system and then put her hand on her earpiece. A few minutes passed and then she smiled.

"We've received confirmation," she said, looking over at her bodyguards.

"Good. So, I'm assuming to you'll send the bust to the address provided," Victoria said, ready to leave.

The woman stopped smiling. Her pale face showed lines around her mouth as she bit her lip. It was obviously a continual facial expression.

"No, I don't think they deliver where you'll be going," she said, pulling out her gun.

***

"It's almost over now," Dmitry said to his men as he led them out of his suite.

He had just received word that his son was safely in the car and headed to the yacht. The bankers had confirmed that the transaction was complete. Now, he could handle this last bit of personal business. Buttoning his suit as he walked, he bypassed the elevators and took the stairs with his men down to the gala floor. He heard the beautiful music playing. Violins rang in his ears. How beautiful that God would let him hear his favorite instrument before the battle of his life. It gave him strength.

Dmitry's foot touched the final step when his men pushed the doors opened for him. They entered into Mezzanine level of the hotel and walked into the ball, where women swayed in beautiful dresses and men led in handsome tuxedos. He was undeniable in this setting. People looked on entranced. Who was the tall giant? He was so stately. So beautiful. The luster of the attention had worn old many years ago for him. He ignored it all.

Concentrating, he scanned the room for Russian military types. There was only one. A slender man with a pointy little nose and high cheek bones in military dress uniform. He stood with a group of other men, obviously body-guards.

It was customary after a deal had been made on this scale for the heads of the organizations to meet once in a amicable setting. The ball was the perfect place. Lots of people. No cops.

They made eye contact, and the small man nodded at him. Dmitry made his way over with his men, and they all left through the back doors that led up a few flights of stairs to a private room overlooking the city.

"I've been waiting for two weeks to meet you," the man said, offering his hand. "And finally."

"Finally," Dmitry said, looking around. "So, I've heard that you're retiring."

"*Posle mnogih let*," the man said, tilting his head proudly.

"Well, *Dolgaya zhizn' dlya vas*," Dmitry said, offering his hand.

"You know, this is where the night gets *interesting*. I could walk right out of here and not tell you what's coming, or I can tell you everything, and *you* stand a chance to stay alive."

Dmitry's face did not change. "I'm listening."

"I only tell you this because the man, *my liaison*, has not been paid his final fee, and it is a hefty one. So, I stand to gain something if he were not around to collect. Also, even though he is efficient, he's not Russian. He's a *Pushkin*. Black men still seeking upward mobility," he laughed.

Dmitry did not.

"A black man? His name wouldn't be Dorian would it?" Dmitry asked.

"It would. I'm not sure what he's planning, but I can assure you that it's not going to be good for you."

"No, I don't think that it will be." Dmitry slipped his hands into his pockets. "Well, it was nice to have met you, *but as you said*, you probably shouldn't be here when he arrives."

"Good luck," the man said, waving his men to collect him. "And a pleasure doing business with you."

***

Dorian walked through the large crowds in the masquerade ball with his mask, scanning the room for threats. One could never be sure who all was with Dmitry, but he had an idea that his numbers were large tonight. He and his crew of ten slipped into the back when they saw their client leave, smiling from ear to ear and talking to his men. They gave a final nod to each other as they passed.

When they walked into the room, Dorian expected Dmitry to be surprised to see him or at least alert, but Dmitry sat on a lounge chair drinking another glass of vodka and talking to his men with his legs crossed and his jacket open.

His man closed the door behind them when they had all filed in. No need to include the outside world in old world business.

"Dmitry Medlov," Dorian said with a kind of condescending smile. "It's been *what*...years?"

"At least three," Dmitry said, not bothering to stand. "Would you like a drink?" he asked, raising his glass.

"I don't drink. You know that."

"Right." Dmitry put down his glass on the table. "The whole holy man act. Won't drink alcohol. Won't curse. Won't eat certain meats, *which you are missing out on by the way*. But *will* have a married woman up to your hotel room for 37 minutes and 12 seconds." Dmitry clenched his jaw and uncrossed his long legs.

"You are thorough, Dmitry. Always have been...and long winded. So let's keep this short and simple."

"Let's." Dmitry stood up. His men stood with him, guns visible.

"Are we going to continue a war that's older than your beautiful, young wife, *or* are we going to move on?" Dorian asked as his men assembled around him.

"Depends. Have you done anything at all besides speaking with my wife that could endanger my family?"

"No."

"Sure about that?" Dmitry tilted his head. "Nothing at all?"

"No," Dorian answered flatly.

"You know, meetings like this are the kind where someone doesn't leave alive," Dmitry reminded Dorian. He pulled his jacket open to reveal his guns. He was doubly strapped with two desert eagles.

"This is true, *brat*."

"I. Am. Not. Your. Brother." Dmitry said, pointing at him with a heart stopping scowl.

***

Royal arrived at the will call and picked up her ticket marked Ms. Stone and headed into the ball. Under dim strobe lights and loud music with people dancing around her, she looked on confused about where to go.

Dorian told her that they would be meeting in a private room. She wondered if she was in the right place. Closing her eyes, she drowned out the music and tried to remember his words, his voice. Then suddenly, she felt a hand on her shoulder. A short man in a Russian uniform smiled at her.

"There in the back, dear," he said, pointing towards the exit sign in the back of the room. "I'm sure they are waiting on you."

She smiled and clenched her fists. Mouthing *thank you*, she slipped through the crowd before

Dmitry's men could get to her and ran through the corridor, up the stairs to the back room. Grasping the cold knob, she opened the door and entered.

Dmitry stood on one side with his men and Dorian stood on the opposite side with his. The men at the door looked on confused. Obviously, they were with Dorian.

"Royal," Dmitry said unsurprised. "Come here. I was hoping that you would miss our little party tonight."

She looked over at Dorian.

"Come here!" Dmitry shouted, making her jump. "Now!"

"No," she said, standing at the door. "Dorian promised a truce. If you would just forgive him for the past." Her eyes were wide and naïve.

Dorian smiled. "A truce," he repeated.

"There can be no *truce*," Dmitry said, raising his hand and motioning for her to come to him. "There is no truce."

"Please, Dmitry. Please," she begged. She walked towards the middle of the floor.

"Do you see his unwillingness to compromise?" Dorian taunted, walking toward her.

"Make one more move, Dorian," Dmitry said calmly. "One more."

Dorian stopped in his tracks only inches away from Royal.

Unexpectedly, Dmitry snatched off his jacket. Everyone looked over at him. What did he expect to do? Fight for her? There was more at stake than her honor.

Dmitry pealed out of his white dress shirt to reveal a bomb strapped to his body. It barely covered the many Vory tattoos and the rippling, angry muscles, covered in venom-pumping veins.

The room was a silent roar.

Check mate.

"Recognize anything familiar, Dorian?" Dmitry asked, pulling his knives from his side, ready to do battle.

"No, Dmitry!" Royal said, trying to run towards him. The men stopped her. "What are you doing?"

"This is the kind of man he is, Royal," Dorian explained. "If it cannot be *his* way, it cannot be...period! He would rather kill us all – kill you. He's an animal."

"This is the bomb you placed on my plane to kill *my* family just yesterday," Dmitry explained more for Royal than Dorian. "I have de-cided....you will not have her, rape her, harm her. I allowed it to happen once. It will not happen ever again. Before she is ruined, I will kill us all. And most of all, you will not have the chance to get to my child!" Dmitry screamed.

"Dmitry..."Royal said confused.

"Do you not realize that you are not safe with this man? He is only committed to the Vory. He always has been. It's why he lied to you about his return. It's why he married you falsely, under a different name, because legally you are not married at all, and he is still within the coveted code that means more to him than *you*. I bought you here to see for yourself, Royal."

Royal looked over at her husband and felt faint. It had never dawned on her that he had staged her death to marry her fraudulently. The pain of the truth stabbed through her like the knives Ivan had used to try to kill her.

"What about the truce?" she asked. She looked over at Dorian for answers.

"He is right about one thing. There can be no truce," Dorian explained. His face changed. He no longer looked trusting. "Because he will never stop and I will never forgive."

"He planted it on our jet, Royal. He plans nothing more than to eliminate our family, and if you are not compliant to eliminate you," Dmitry said, standing strong. "Look around, Dorian. While your men scatter at the very sight of this contraption that you yourself built, my men are ready to die...to stop this now. And we *will* die. I came here to stop you for good. And as much as I love my wife, if I have to take her with me to stop this, I will. You will not have her or my daughter or my son. You will not destroy another life like did with your half-sister, Ari."

Royal put her hands on her head and looked down at the floor. So that was the connection. Ivan's dead wife was Dorian's sister. It would explain why Ivan was sexually fixated with her. It would explain why Dorian wanted her here. It would explain why this had to end, why it would not stop. She sighed.

"I didn't destroy her. You did when sent Ivan to kill me, when you killed her, when you killed your own brother," Dorian shot back.

"So much of a holy man, yet so out for revenge," Dmitry noted. "Hypocrite."

"An eye for an eye, Dmitry," Dorian said. "If it's of any consequence, I have no plans of hurting her. And I think I'll make a fine father."

Falling to her knees, Royal cried out.

"You lied to me, Dmitry. You said you that you would never return," she said on the ground in tears. "Now look at all that you've caused again!"

"I am sorry, my love. I only did this for the family. I had no desire to return."

"Why couldn't you just walk away?"

"Did you think if this deal went down, even if I did not participate that it would not affect our family? This is about him and his vendetta."

"You lied to me," she cried. "You lied!"

Dorian walked over to her. He placed a hand on her exposed shoulder. He felt for the confused woman. She had been doubly deceived.

It was never his intention to form a truce. It was only his intention to expose Dmitry as Ivan had failed to do and take her away from the life that she hated, where she was guarded and unable to even have her own name. Plus, it was an eye for an eye. A wife for a wife. A life for a life.

"I will give you the life that you deserve," he said softly to Royal. "You and your beautiful daughter. I will listen to you. I. Will. Love. You.," he said convincingly. "I will not deny you a full existence. He will. Can't you see that now?"

The sight infuriated Dmitry beyond control. He howled out. "How dare you! I will kill the very thought of you! This is my country! This is my shit! That is my fucking wife! And you, you are not without blame. You have killed, murdered, destroyed no differently than me. Now you feel entitled to my life?" He foamed at the mouth like a mad dog. "The only mistake I ever made was not killing you myself, but I'll rectify it tonight."

Dmitry's men prepared to strike, guns pointed, eyes focused. The other men scurried to the door, some snuck out quietly, running away from a sure detonation.

"I will blow this entire city to high fucking hell, and I will laugh as I do it before I let you take her and destroy her anymore than she has already been harmed by my sick-ass brother, or your whore of sister, or my own sins."

"Ah, now the truth comes out, brother." Dorian laughed. "You are jealous."

"You and Ivan were a monstrosity!" Dmitry screamed. "The both of you! Worthless men who would hide their hand after throwing a rock. Scared little boys, the both of you. Both unworthy of living. Well, one is dead. One is left."

"Stop," Royal cried.

"And you the big bad wolf that never hid anything but his money. How are you so different?"

"When I kill a man, I do it face-to-face. I never hide behind bomb. I never hide my fucking hand."

"But you could so easily hide everything else," Dorian countered. "Even from the woman that you claim to love."

"He's right, Dmitry," Royal cried. "I'm tired of being something that I'm not. You lied. How can I trust again? We are not even married. I am a fraud. This marriage is a fraud. This man has offered me peace. He has offered me a new life. And you would rather kill me than see me happy."

Dorian smiled. He was happy to have her feed in although she was so terribly wrong.

"Royal?" Dmitry whispered her named. "Royal, what are you saying? Do you know what he will do to you? He will destroy you. He will destroy our child, our dreams. I love you. You are my wife. You are my entire world!"

"Lies! All lies!" she screamed.

Still on her knees, she placed her hands firmly on the ground under the bottom of her long, flowing black dress and rocked herself while Dorian looked over at Dmitry, satisfied with how her words had dismantled him. She cried aloud, cried for the pain, cried for the rape, cried for her daughter, cried until she was nearly invisible in the room.

"That's it, motherfucker," Dmitry said, headed for him.

Dorian welcomed it. He braced himself for the rush.

Then sly, curled up on the floor, Royal pulled the gun from under her dress and quickly pulled the trigger. She felt the jerk of the powerful weapon push her backwards. It happened so fast until she was not even certain that she had hit her target. It pained her to look.

Before Dorian could look back down at her, he heard the loud explosion. It was the first of many shots. People dropped around the room in a blink of an eye as men pointed their guns and aimed. The clicks of machinery filled the room. In slow motion, Dorian looked down at his stomach to find blood spewing from his would.

He fell to his knees behind her in dismay. Rubbing his hands over his injury, he collapsed on the hard floor with his eyes focused in on her.

"Hiding you hand is always a bad thing," Royal said, shooting him once more. Blood splattered on her face and across the room.

Around her, bullets whizzed. Again déjà vu. She curled up by the dead man to take cover and looked across the room as her husband attacked Dorian's men in a full animalistic rage.

Guns blazing, Dmitry's men ripped through the remainder of Dorian's men, while he slaughtered them with his knives, slicing them open with quick wrists movements and angry punches. Dropping the knives, he stood like a mountain in his place, Desert Eagle guns in both hands pumping bullets into the walls, blasting the glass and killing them all.

She saw the satisfaction in his face. The completion of his act was startling. Her husband was a monster, but she loved him. And he had only returned for her. She knew that. She knew him, regardless of what some stranger told her.

She heard heavy footsteps running towards her. Closing her eyes to prepare for whatever would come, she felt Dmitry land on top of her, still shooting and protecting her.

He finally stood in the silent room, all of Dorian's men dead, some of Dmitry's as well. He picked Royal up in his arms, scooped her up from the floor with Dorian's blood drenching the train of her dress. Dropping the disengaged bomb from his body onto Dorian's chest, he quickly hurried out in the hotel.

The gun shots alarmed the people dancing carefree at the ball in the adjourning room. They heard the screams and saw the men running out covered in blood creating mass hysteria. Hundreds of people flooded out of the ballroom, trampling over their masks and pushing each other to get away from apparent doom as security pushed through unsuccessfully to get towards the backroom.

Dmitry, Royal and his men blended in with the crowd as they ran quickly out of the building and loaded into their cars.

***

The deal was complete. The cargo was moved by the Spetsnaz from its safe location in Sochi to cargo boats outside of the city on the waterway that would drop the goods off across the Black Sea in Istanbul with a very eager group of Jewish freedom fighters coming up from Israel to meet him. His father had done it. He had made Anatoly a living legend. Only at what cost?

Still in his tux, Anatoly sat on Bardzecki's yacht alone looking out across the dark water as the fireworks were set off on the pier. The vibrant colors lit up the skyline with vivid hues of happiness. He looked up in a daze recalling his father's advise for the hundredth time. His father had warned him, but he had ignored him. Don't send her, if you care for her. Now, he was alone on the yacht with no word from Victoria.

He told her to meet him immediately after. A small speed boat would bring her from the shore to the yacht, and she would travel with him to Istanbul, maybe do some shopping in the Grand Bazaar and definitely a quick stop in the art district of Nuruosmaniye Caddesi to get rid of the hideous bust he had bought tonight for $550 million.

Only, when he called her phone, it went straight to voicemail – a definite sign that something was wrong, possibly horribly wrong.

For the life of him he could not understand why Victoria meant anything at all to him. He had tried to rationalize how losing her would be a good thing, how sending her into harms way would show how much he despised her. Yet, he found himself spending far too much thinking about the simplest words she said or the looks that she gave him. In just a couple of days, he had become bewitched, though he would never admit it. Maybe he wouldn't have to.

He took a sip from his drink and looked out across the waterway at the city moving farther and farther away.

Chapter 22

A beautiful sunset casted a tranquil glow over the Medlov Chateau as the family prepared for a huge dinner for the family and staff. A month had passed since *the Dorian incident,* and things were finally back to normal.

Royal and Dmitry had committed to being completely transparent, and Anatoly had been off for a month selling his inventory around the world. Anya had even started to attend a school in town only blocks from the boutique that Royal and Dmitry drove her to and picked her up from every day.

Tonight, the feast was larger than ever. Food had been prepared all day, and the house was cleaned and opened in celebration of Dmitry and Royal's newest addition to the Medlov Family scheduled to arrive in eight months.

The news had come as shocker weeks after the two arrived back from Sochi in the form of morning sickness for Royal. Dmitry was ecstatic at the prospect of *doing it right this time*, and they quickly headed to the doctor for confirmation and prenatal care.

Royal's enormous appetite had Dmitry cooking constantly. He prepared special meals for her every day at the restaurant and spent his nights picking out names and preparing the nursery, which adjoined to Anya's bedroom. For the family, this was their third chance at a new life, and they intended to succeed this time.

The dinner had already started when Anatoly arrived. He came in with bags of gifts for everyone and doggy treats for Anya's puppy. The family had all but begged him to fly in.

Since Sochi, he seemed very much removed from everyone, always working and never spending time with the family anymore. Dmitry knew that it was because of Victoria. Only, every time that he dared broach the topic, Anatoly only withdrew more. It took Anya calling to invite him to the party for him to come. He could never resist his little sister.

His blonde locks mirrored his fathers. They had both grown their hair back, only Anatoly had also grown a full beard. His tanned face was aged slightly, and he had a permanent scowl.

"Anatoly!" Anya screamed when she saw him. She ran across the foyer and jumped in his arms.

Dropping the bags, he quickly picked her up and swung her around, glad to see his favorite girl. "How are you, baby?" he asked, kissing her rosy cheeks. "I've missed you so much."

"We've missed you, too," she said as he put her down. "Where have you been?"

"Around," he said, rubbing through her hair. "I brought all these beautiful pink boxes just for you. They are full of gifts from around the globe, *even* from Disneyworld."

Her face lit up. "Oh, thank you. Thank you, Anatoly," she said, hugging him.

Royal rounded the corner slightly pudgy and glowing. She extended her arms and hugged him warmly. Rubbing his beard, she kissed his cheek and grabbed his hand.

"I was hoping that you would show," she said, guiding him to the dining hall. "Everyone is already here."

"I'm sure that no one came to see me," he said gruffly. "You look great. Big and pregnant."

"Shut up," she said laughing.

"No, the look fits you. You should stay knocked up."

They entered into the main dining hall to see all the staff from the house, the restaurant and the boutique along with acquaintances of Dmitry and Royal at the various tables eating, drinking and talking.

All eyes went to Anatoly as he walked through the door with Royal. As usual the women swooned and whispered about him. A month ago, he would have taken a mental note of each and everyone one, but tonight he simply made his way to his father's table.

Dmitry stood and gave him a hug. They laughed and embraced each other, and then Dmitry offered him a seat.

"Good to see you, son. How's life?"

"Busy, papa. Good to see you, too."

Dmitry wiped his mouth with his napkin and gave a clever grin. He looked over at Royal and winked his eye.

"I have brought special wine from my last trip to Italy. Why don't you go into kitchen and grab it for me?"

"Wine? Papa, I'm boss now. Why do you send me to do these types of things?"

"Because it is from the new winery that I just purchased last week. I already have someone running it, but I'd like for you to sample it. Tell me if you like it."

"Alright," he sighed. "Where is it?"

"I left it on countertop."

"What it is called? I'm sure that there is more than one bottle in kitchen, old man." He was almost short with his father.

"It's called *donna bella*."

"Beautiful woman?"

"Yes, you like?" Dmitry's eyes were eager.

"That's not very original, papa" he said, standing up. "I'll be right back."

Anatoly made his way through the crowds of people, past the servers to the kitchen. He walked in and looked to the long island in front of the door and grabbed the bottle. Sure enough. A bottle of *Donna Bella* was sitting there waiting for him.

He picked it up and looked at the bottle. It *was* sort of a catchy name now that he thought about it, and the label was impressive with gold foil and crimson and green colors. Okay, maybe he was being too hard on the old man.

"What are you drinking?" a voice asked, behind him in the corner.

Anatoly looked up from the bottle but wouldn't turn around.

"Wine," he clenched his jaw.

He heard the click of heels behind him, moving towards him slowly. He could feel the sway of her hips even before he could see her.

"Chardonnay? What year?" the voice asked.

Anatoly turned slowly to find Victoria standing behind him in a pair of skinny jeans that showed her bo-legs and stilettos that made her even taller. Her long hair was pulled into a ponytail, and she sported large diamond studs. She gave a big smile and blushed slightly at the look on his face.

She took the bottle from him and grabbed the two glasses waiting beside it. Pouring him a glass, she handed it to him.

"I'm doing you the courtesy of not sneaking it to you like a fucking snake. Now drink it," she mocked.

Anatoly took the glass and drank all of the wine then pulled her into him. They looked at each other for a long while in the silence of the kitchen. She ran her hands through his curly locks and down through his scruffy beard, and he held her close clenching her waist and thighs.

"I thought you were dead," he confessed.

"Your father has a very long reach. The woman who worked for Dorian was paid off the day of the event by Dmitry to get me to Kerch."

"Kerch?"

"Yeah, I'd never been there before. Anyway, this woman pulls a gun on me, then escorts me out the back of the studio after the transaction had been made. The next day, I ended up in Kerch. I was there for weeks, and then I went to Yalta." She shrugged her shoulders. "The Ukraine is really a pretty place."

"Some parts of it. My father told me that he had friends in Kerch."

"Yeah, some pretty heavy hitters, too. I stayed there until he sent for me, and then I ended up in Italy at a damned winery. Your father was there talking to some Italian guy in Italian. So, I didn't even know what they were saying. Then he offered me a job to work there, market his stuff, you know legit work. He bought the damned winery that day, and I got a sweet job. It's nice."

"Why didn't you call me?"

"I wanted to, but Dmitry and Royal insisted that I did not. They said to get my life straight first, make sure the heat was off of that *last thing*, because it was all over the world news and everything, and then when it was time, I could see you again."

Anatoly looked down at the ground. "I should have never sent you there."

"It's the best thing you have done. Really," she lifted his chin.

"So you're not a deviant anymore?"

"Oh, yeah," she laughed. "I'm just not setting up old rich guys anymore. I sell wine," she laughed. "But I've missed you."

He leaned against the island and pulled him to her. "Missed you."

"Are you hungry?"

"Not really."

"Want to get out here. Maybe go to the condo?" she asked. "It has been a month."

Anatoly patted his pockets. "I've got my keys right here. Let's go."

"What about saying goodbye to your folks?"

"My father said goodbye when he sent me in here," he smiled. "I'll catch him in the morning."

The two left quickly towards the garage while the rest of the family ate dinner together and laughed and sang while the band played an upbeat Russian tune.

Snacking on a pickle, Royal looked towards the door to see if anyone was coming. "I guess he found the *wine*," she laughed.

"I guess so," Dmitry shook his head. He pulled her to him and kissed her lips. "I love you."

"I love you, too," she said, touching his face.

"What about *me*?" Anya asked.

"We love you, too," they both said, pulling her over to them.

The End

Send your feedback today to
Latrivia@LatriviaNelson.com!

Dmitry's Closet (2010)

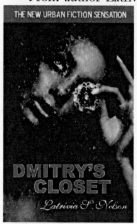

From author Latrivia S. Nelson, author of the epic romance *Ivy's Twisted Vine*, comes a story about Memphis, TN, a deadly faction of the Russian mafia and an innocent woman who dismantles an empire. Orphaned virgin Royal Stone is looking for employment in one of the country's toughest recessions. What she finds is the seven-foot, blonde millionaire Dmitry Medlov, who offers her a job as the manager of his new boutique Dmitry's Closet. After she accepts his job offer, she soon accepts his gifts, his bed and his lifestyle. What she does not know is that her knight in shining armor is also the head of the Medlov Organized Crime Family, a faction of the elite Russian mafia Vory v Zakone. Falling in love with the clueless Royal makes Dmitry want to break the code, leave his empire and start a life far away from the perils of the Thieves-in-Law. Only, his brother Ivan comes to the Memphis from New York City bent on a murderous revenge. With the FBI and Memphis Police Department working hard to build a case against Dmitry and his brother trying to kill him, he is forced to tell Royal of his true identity, but Royal also is keeping a secret - one that changes everything. Who will win? Who will lose? Who will die? Watch all the skeletons as they tumble out of the urban literature sensation Dmitry's Closet.

www.dmitryscloset.com

The Medlov Crime Family Series

About the Author

Latrivia S. Nelson is an urban fiction and interracial romance author. Her first novel, Ivy's Twisted Vine (2008), is the largest interracial novel in its genre. Dmitry's Closet is her first urban fiction/interracial romance novel and a bestseller.

Currently, Nelson is working on her next book and pursing her Ph.D. in criminal justice. She lives in the suburbs of Memphis with her husband (Adam) and two children (Tierra & Jordan) and is a senior specialist for The Carter Malone Group, a full-service public relations firm.

"Typically, I write about untraditional, unconventional and taboo relationships in contemporary society. I give them a voice, and they give me inspiration. So far, I've never conformed, and I probably never will."

-Latrivia S. Nelson
www.latrivianelson.com

LaVergne, TN USA
26 August 2010
194789LV00001B/7/P